Fortune's Fools

Fortune's Fools

Julia Parks

THORNDIKE
CHIVERS

This Large Print edition is published by Thorndike Press®,
Waterville, Maine USA and by BBC Audiobooks, Ltd,
Bath, England.

Published in 2004 in the U.S. by arrangement with
Zebra Books, an imprint of Kensington Publishing Corp.

Published in 2004 in the U.K. by arrangement with
the author.

U.S. Hardcover 0-7862-6784-4 (Romance)
U.K. Hardcover 1-4056-3052-3 (Chivers Large Print)

The text of this Large Print edition is unabridged.
Other aspects of the book may vary from the original edition.

Set in 16 pt. Plantin by Myrna S. Raven.

Printed in the United States on permanent paper.

British Library Cataloguing-in-Publication Data available

Library of Congress Cataloging-in-Publication Data

Parks, Julia.
    Fortune's fools / Julia Parks.
       p. cm.
    ISBN 0-7862-6784-4 (lg. print : hc : alk. paper)
    1. London (England) — Fiction.   2. Irish — England —
Fiction.   3. Large type books.   I. Title.
PS3616.A756F67 2004
813'.6—dc22   2004050142

For Vicki and Bill, David and Jan,
Nick and Barbara, Steve and Judy,
with love.

One

"And this time, you must find yourselves wives! You cannot forever live off your brother's bounty!"

"Really, Papa, Max and Tristram are always welcome here at Darwood Hall," said Montgomery, heir to the dissolute Viscount Tavistoke.

"I'll wager your bride does not agree with that," snapped his father.

The bride in question entered the drawing room and went to her new husband's side, slipping her arm around his waist. "What would I not agree with, Papa Tavistoke?"

Her husband's twin, Maxwell, said, "Papa says you don't want us about anymore, me or Tris."

"I hate to disagree with you, Papa Tavistoke, but you must know that I enjoy having all of you living here at Darwood Hall. My goodness, just because I have wed your son, that does not mean I wish to change the family. This is their home, too," said Clarissa, earning an approving grin from her husband and her two brothers-in-law.

The youngest Darby brother, who was more attuned to the feelings of others, said quickly, "You are wonderful, Clarissa, but it is not right for Max and me to hang about the estate now that you are here. When you and Monty have been wed a year or more, you will be looking for any opportunity to be rid of us." As he spoke, he smiled slightly, his pale blue eyes twinkling.

"I would never do that, Tris," she replied, shaking her head.

Maxwell Darby rose and smiled at her, saying, "Yes, you will, and while I might like staying here, especially now that you are here to make certain the meals are decent and the house is clean, it is not fair to saddle you with all of us at once."

"But, Max, this is your home, too," said his brother.

"Yes, it will always be home, but Tris and I have our own places."

Their new sister-in-law exclaimed in horror, "Oh, Max, you cannot possibly mean to move there. The roofs have caved in and there is . . ."

"No, no, but we don't have the means to fix them. That is why we are going to do as our reprobate father has suggested and return to London for the Little Season to secure our own brides."

"Heiresses," corrected his father, rubbing his hands together gleefully. "Isn't it lucky that I haven't put my hands on the funds to repay the marquess?"

His entire family gaped at his outrageous interpretation of their financial state. Ignoring their shock, the viscount continued, "Otherwise, he might not have agreed to foot the bill for yet another visit to London, and you boys might not have the chance to win your heiresses."

"Heiresses, Papa? Tris and I can only endeavor to find wives who are capable of helping out, shall we say, when it comes to repairing those houses and putting our small estates in order," said Max.

"Do not forget paying off the marquess so he doesn't have me thrown into gaol," said their sire.

Tristram, who was looking decidedly stubborn, declared, "I might endeavor, but I'll be dashed if I will saddle myself with some antidote just because she has money. Only look at Monty and how happy he is with our Clarissa. How can you think of settling for anything less, Max?"

"How sweet of you," said his brother's bride, crossing over to Tristram, standing on tiptoe, and kissing his smooth cheek.

He blushed and stammered, "I . . . you're welcome, Clarissa."

"Tristram's right, Papa. We'll go to London, and we will do our best. That's all we can do," said Max, his dark blue eyes challenging his father to dispute his words.

"Bah! Your best just might not . . . wait a minute." His eyes narrowing slightly, the viscount snapped his fingers and smiled at each of his listeners. "We leave first thing in the morning."

"We!" exclaimed all three of his sons.

"Yes. If I am there, I can make certain you meet the right type of girl before falling for the wrong type of girl! There's no reason the girl you settle on should *not* be worth a fortune, is there?" With this, the old man toddled out of the room, happily rubbing his hands again.

"I do not envy you this visit," said Montgomery, grinning at his brothers. "You will probably be unable to find any sort of wife because you will be forced to look after Papa from dusk to dawn, keeping him out of the gambling hells and worse."

"An impossible task," muttered Max. "He'll not be content until we are, all of us, in debtor's gaol."

"Barton, you old dog, it is good to see

you," said Max, offering his hand to their former servant as he stepped across the threshold of the modest house their benefactor had lent them for the Little Season.

Barton ignored the hand and began removing Max's coat instead. "It is gratifying to see you in good health, Master Max," said the manservant. "You, too, Master Tristram."

"Thank you, Barton," said the youngest Darby brother. "I hope the marquess did not make you too miserable while we were gone."

"Oh, no, sir. His lordship was quite generous. I was allowed to keep his house in London running smoothly while he went to the country for the summer."

"Spent the summer in London?" said Max. "Whew, I would not call that generous."

"No, no, as I said he was quite generous. As an alternative, he offered to, uh, release me from my obligation altogether."

"He was going to let you go after all these years? The bastard."

"Now, now, Master Max. Please remember, I am under an obligation to his lordship," said the servant, handing each of them a glass of port.

Max gave an impatient snort. "Yes, yes,

you slept with his mistress, but how long is he going to hold that against you? I mean, how many has he had since that one? She could not have mattered all that much!"

"I . . . well, never mind that. Summer is past, and you are back in London for me to look after — and this time in a proper house, too. Later, perhaps, if one of you should succeed in wedding an heiress . . . but tell me, how have your clothes fared without me to look after them?"

"We're sorry, Barton, but . . ."

The servant paled and put his hand to his mouth. Just then, their driver kicked open the door and shoved a trunk through the opening.

"Be careful with that!" exclaimed Barton, rushing to supervise the disposition of their trunks. When Max and Tristram were alone, they grinned at each other.

"We should not provoke him so," said Tristram. "He nearly had an apoplexy over our wardrobes."

"I was only having a bit of a go at him. He'll find out soon enough that we haven't touched our London attire since we went home last June. Still, Tris, we must do something for old Barton."

"Do something? The best thing we can

do is to wed our heiresses and give him a new position, away from the dirty marquess," said Tristram, flopping onto the sofa and putting his booted feet on one end before folding his arms behind his head to cradle it.

"All the more reason for us to redouble our efforts," said Max, dropping into a chair by the fire and leaning forward to warm his hands. "We must succeed where Monty failed."

"Failed to wed a harridan, you mean. I am delighted he chose Clarissa over her cousin."

"Of course, we are all delighted, but again, that is all the more reason to secure our fortunes. We'll be able to share with Monty and Clarissa, too. They are going to fill their nursery with children before they know it, and they will not have a penny to put bread in their mouths."

"You are exaggerating now," said Tristram. "Monty has invested some of the money the marquess gave them as a wedding present. They'll not starve."

"No, but there is not enough to perform all the repairs and improvements Darwood Hall so desperately needs," came Max's gloomy reply.

"True, true. Still, Max, I shall sell some

more drawings, and I've . . . but there, I mustn't count on too much from . . . well, from my work."

"Fixing up those run-down properties that Papa calls our inheritance is going to take more than your little drawings, Tristram. And what about Papa?"

"Yes, there are always Papa's vowels, which the marquess still holds — the real reason we have been dragged down to this. I know Cravenwell was not quite as dastardly as we thought, but I cannot forget his threat to have Papa thrown into debtor's prison — and him Papa's oldest friend, too."

"What a coil the old man has brought us to," muttered Max. "I will never gamble with money I don't have."

"Oh? What about last spring?"

"That was different. It was not money. It was Thunderlight, and, as I told Monty and Clarissa when they found out, there was no chance that Thunderlight would lose those races. Therefore, it was not really gambling."

"No chance?" teased Tristram.

"No, I always made certain . . ."

"Master Max, Master Tristram! Thank you! Thank you!" said Barton, hurrying in from the bedrooms. "Everything is just as I

14

sent it home with you! You haven't worn any of them since you left me! Bless you."

Grinning, Max rose and said, "Only what we have on our backs. Speaking of which, I would dearly love a bath after two days on the road. And then I want my riding gear. I've a mind to put Thunderlight through his paces." Barton's face crumpled, and Max grabbed the servant by the lapels and demanded, "What is it, man? Has something happened to Thunderlight?"

It was Max's turn to pale as the servant looked away, unable to meet his eyes.

"The marquess . . . after you left, he continued to race Thunderlight. He had his groom, Needham, ride him. I'm afraid . . . he lost him to some Irish horse breeder. I . . . I am sorry, Master Max."

"When did it happen?"

"Not more than three weeks ago."

"Then he might still be in London. Perhaps I can buy . . ." Max looked from the servant to his brother and dropped his head in despair. "Money. It is always a matter of money." With this, he grabbed his hat and slammed out of the room.

"I had better go after him," said Tristram, unfolding his long legs and rising.

"Tell him I am sorry, sir."

"I'll tell him, but it will not cheer him. When Max gets blue deviled, there is no jostling him free of it. And this, after all, is about a horse. There is nothing as important to Max as his horses."

Tristram settled his hat on his unfashionably long blond hair and headed after his impetuous brother. At four and twenty, Tristram Darby was maturing into a fine figure of a man. His lanky frame had filled out during the summer in the country as he enjoyed his new sister-in-law's menus. Long rambles through the woods, looking for inspiration for his writing, had left him fit and muscular. The combination of his blue eyes and broad shoulders now rendered him a handsome man, where the previous Season he had been only a youth.

Following his equally handsome brother with no difficulty, Tristram traversed the street and soon found himself nearing the park. Still, Max's strides did not falter. Into the park and across the green grass he marched until he came to an ornamental pond. Here, Max stopped, kicked up a pebble at his feet, stooped down to retrieve it, and skipped it across the glassy surface. Pebble after pebble followed.

After watching for several minutes,

Tristram asked, "Does that help?"

Max turned and scowled at him before shaking his head. "All summer, all I thought about was Thunderlight and how I might somehow buy him. When Papa mentioned returning to London, I came because Thunderlight was here, not because I wanted to find a wife."

"I know," said Tristram. His tone offered sympathy, but he did not bother to spout platitudes. Both of them knew that the horse was out of Max's reach — probably forever. It was a devastating blow. Max loved horses better than life itself, and Thunderlight above all. If the marquess had not lost the stallion, at least Max would have been able to ride him.

Tristram clapped his brother on the back. "Come on, Max. You'll feel better after you've cleaned up. We'll go to Manton's and . . ." His words were cut short by the thundering sound of hooves breaking the stillness of the morning.

"What the devil?" exclaimed Max, whirling around to watch as Thunderlight — his Thunderlight — broke free of the trees, the mighty horse's hooves churning up the turf as he raced toward the park gates. Max started forward, only to have his steps falter.

"It's a . . . girl! Devil take me! It's a blasted girl!"

They watched as the stallion came to a plunging halt, and the black-clad figure clinging to his neck sat up, straightened her mannish shako hat, and rode calmly out of the park gates.

Max sprang into action, and Tristram called after him, "Where the deuce are you going?"

"I've got to catch her up!" he called over his shoulder as his legs began to fly, carrying him swiftly toward the gates. He was so caught up in the pursuit, he narrowly missed being run down by a small carriage. Dodging its wheels, Max continued on, leaving Tristram to grin after him.

Tristram's amusement faded as he focused on the carriage and its occupant, a large, round female in purple and black. Frowning, Tristram saw the flutter of a yellow sleeve. Odd, he thought. His eyes widened as the yellow sleeve's owner leaned forward, her golden hair shining in the sunlight, her delicate features etching themselves in his mind as the carriage plodded past.

When they were gone, Tristram expelled a pent-up breath. That was undoubtedly the most beautiful little face he had ever seen. Taking out his notebook, he wandered along the path, following the carriage as he penned an ode in tribute to the unknown girl's exquisite beauty. When he found a secluded spot, he flung himself on the ground and began to sketch her face, his pencil flying as he captured the unknown girl's beauty with his skilled hand.

Tilting his head to one side, Tristram Darby smiled. He would need his paints to do her beauty justice. Setting aside his drawing, he flipped to a fresh page and began writing.

The morning turned into afternoon, and still he wrote. Noise finally broke his concentration, and Tristram looked up at the sun, frowning in surprise to find it sitting on top of the trees. Where had the time gone? The park was no longer the quiet haven it had been in the morning.

Clambering to his feet, Tristram put away his pencil and paper and strolled toward the entrance, pleased with his work for the day. After a quick walk back to their house, he opened the small secretary and picked up his pen, repairing the point before copying his hastily written notes onto larger paper, adding each page to a larger stack. An hour later, with a flourish, he wrote "The End" and sat back, a wide grin on his face.

"Oh, Master Tristram. I did not realize you had returned. Could I bring you something to eat or drink?" asked Barton.

"No, thank you, Barton. I must go out again," he replied, rising and picking up the stack of papers. He straightened it and tied it with a string. "I will probably not be back for supper, either."

"Very good, sir."

Tristram tucked the money purse into his coat pocket and said good-bye before leaving the large, messy office.

"Mr. Darby, a moment, please," said the man behind the desk, patting the stack of papers in front of him. "What name do you wish to use?"

"The title is there. *Sir Milton's Triumph.*"

"No, I meant as the author, you may wish to use a different name from your own. Most of the gentry don't want anyone knowing they write novels and such. Some just put down 'A Lady of Quality' or simply 'A Gentleman.'"

"I really hadn't considered." Tristram hesitated only a moment.

Recalling how much trouble his drawings had caused when they were published last Season, he certainly did not wish to have another such scandal attached to the Darby name.

"Yes, I think you are right, Mr. Rider. Very well, I shall use the name Richard Poorman. How is that?"

The publisher scratched his head, but he nodded and wrote the name on the first page of Tristram's manuscript. Then he rose and offered his hand to the young gentleman, who took it and shook it once firmly.

"I think Mr. Poorman is going to prove very popular and very profitable for us both, young man."

"I only hope you are right, Mr. Rider. Good day."

"Good day, sir."

Whistling, Tristram left the office and made his way to the door. Drawing all those broadsides the spring before had been profitable, but hardly enough to repair the family fortunes. This book, however, if it did as well as Mr. Rider thought it would, should make it possible for him and his brothers to live a little more comfortably. It wouldn't pay off his father's debts to the Marquess of Cravenwell, but it would be a start.

And perhaps, if this one was popular, he could write another one, and another . . .

Tristram grinned, tipping his hat to a

passing matron. His step jaunty, he proceeded to the coffee house across the street to celebrate the sale of his first novel. He would not tell Max, not yet. He would wait until the book was printed and see how it sold. Perhaps . . . *careful,* he cautioned himself. He did not want to live on daydreams the way his father always had. The next turn of the card was always going to be the big winner for his father. No, Tristram had no desire to be like him. He would keep his feet firmly planted on the ground.

"Mary Katherine O'Connor! Come here this instant! And don't think ye kin be hidin' from me, me fine girl!" The still handsome Kieran O'Connor bounded up the stairs like a man of twenty and threw open his daughter's door.

Feigning surprise, Kate O'Connor exclaimed, "Papa! You should knock before entering a lady's chamber!"

"None of your fine airs wi' me, Mary Kate," he said.

Kate smiled. Things were not so bad if her father was already calling her Mary Kate. Soon, it would be only Kate again, and his temper would be cooled completely.

"Papa, what has happened? It is not Mama, is it?"

"Not . . . o' course not. Your dear mother is fine, like I told you she would be. A mere case of the sniffles. She'll be right as rain in no time and ready to take you to all the balls and such you can handle."

He scowled at the glimmer of amusement in her green eyes and wagged a finger at her, scolding, "None o' your tricks, do you hear? I came up here to tell you what's what. I know you've been out on that stallion, tearing through the streets, making a spectacle o' yourself. You'll send your sainted mother back to her sickbed, you will, if you don't leave behind your hoydenish ways."

"But, Papa, Thunderlight has to have exercise."

"And what do you think I pay Bobby O'Hara for, if not to ride the horses? And not like some sort of banshee."

"Papa, I do not ride like a banshee, though how you could know how they ride, I'm certain I don't know. Have you ever seen a banshee?" She calculated that this last question was enough to make her father forget everything else, and she smiled inwardly when he took the bait.

"A man doesn't have to have seen something, to know that it exists. And don't think they don't exist, because they do. Your mother . . ."

"Kieran, dearest, what is all this clamor about?"

"Mama," said Kate, hurrying to the doorway where her invalid mother was swaying delicately. She led her into the room and saw her seated in front of the fire before ringing for tea.

"Anne, you shouldn't be up and about yet," said her husband, kneeling by her side and patting her hand.

"Nonsense. I am fine, Kieran, and so the doctor told you this morning. Now, what is all this noise about?"

"Nothing, my love, nothing at all."

"You know me and Papa, Mama. We love to squabble, but we did not mean to disturb you," said Kate, bringing a shawl and placing it around her mother's narrow shoulders. She then sat down on the foot-stool, folding her long legs beneath her. Her mother smiled at her and patted her daughter's red curls.

"What have you been doing this morning, my love, that has your father in such a state?"

"Nothing." Kate blushed and grimaced. "Well, not much. I just went for a ride in the park."

"On that black devil," muttered her father.

"He is not a devil," said Kate, her green eyes sparking with defiance and indignation.

"Kieran, can Kate handle him?"

"You know she can," said Kieran O'Connor, his chest swelling with pride. "Our Kate can handle anything on four legs, but that is not the point. She should not be racing through the park, no matter how early in the morning she rides."

"Your father is right, Kate, and you know it, don't you?"

"Yes, Mama," she replied.

"Good. Then it shan't happen again?"

"No, Mama."

"Good. You know, Kate, I do believe I am feeling strong enough to accompany you to the shops this afternoon. You have your first fitting with the seamstress, do you not?"

"That would be wonderful," said Kate, her green eyes meeting her father's. "Are you sure you are well enough?"

"Yes, dear. It's only right that your mother should go with you on such a momentous occasion. Besides, I may run into some old acquaintances, and that will mean more invitations, more balls, and more suitors for you to choose from."

"I . . . yes, Mama."

Anne O'Connor rose with the help of her daughter and husband. Leaning heavily on his arm, she allowed him to lead her to the door where she paused.

"Can you be ready in an hour, my Kate?"

"Yes, Mama. I'll be ready."

The door closed on her parents, and Kate rushed to the bed, flinging herself down on it, her face buried in the pillow while the sobs racked her body.

It was unspoken, the knowledge that her mother would never fully recover her health. It was always there, looming over everyone in the household, that Mrs. O'Connor might not recover this time, from this miscarriage.

When she had discovered that her mother was once more with child, she had raged at her father, calling him a beast and worse. Her mother's quiet reprimand had taken the wind out of her sails. Love, she insisted softly, had a mind of its own, and the baby was simply a result of their love — for each other and for her. How, her mother had whispered, could she not hope for another child like her beloved Kate?

It had ended like the others. Her mother had lost the baby just before coming to

London for her daughter's first Season. The experience had weakened her further, and she had yet to recover. The London physician had confided to Kate and her father that Mrs. O'Connor would likely never be the same, that the weakness might never leave her. Her mother, however, had called the physician a quack and assured them that she would be fine in time.

Kate sat up and dried her tears. After bathing her face in the cool water on the nightstand, she began removing her riding habit. Her mother wanted her to have a Season in London, just as she had done before meeting her Irish rogue of a husband. She was certain her long-legged, full-figured Kate would be a great success.

Gazing candidly at her wild red curls and freckled nose, Kate doubted she would take London by storm. To her own critical eyes, she looked too much like her father, and she was more accustomed to the stable than the drawing room. But for her Mama, she would endure anything.

Making a moue at her image, she turned away and donned her dark red gown with its matching spencer trimmed in gold braid. She loved the gown, which fitted her well and suited her coloring. With a final glance in the glass, she left the room

27

walking down the short corridor to her mother's room to help her down the stairs.

"Your papa ordered the carriage, did he not, Miss Kate?" asked Dolly, her mother's faithful maid.

"Yes, it is waiting at the front door. Is that cloak warm enough, Mama? We do not want you to get a chill."

"Certainly not," said the maid.

"I am fine," insisted Mrs. O'Connor, smiling at them and shaking her head. "Each of you give me an arm on the stairs, and we will manage admirably."

"Yes, Mama," said Kate.

"Yes, madam," said Dolly.

When they were finally settled in the small landaulet, Kate breathed a sigh of relief. The coachman sent the horses down the street, traveling at a sedate pace.

"Papa says you are to have everything I deem necessary," said Mrs. O'Connor.

"Surely we have already ordered everything that is necessary," said Kate.

"No, we have only begun, my dear. A lady must have a different gown for every major ball."

"How silly!" said Kate.

"Well, that is an exaggeration, perhaps. But if you wear the same gown, you must do something different. A different shawl, new ribbons, perhaps another flounce."

"Mama, I know you and Papa . . ."

"Sh, Kate. We have been through it all before. If you had chosen one of the young gentlemen at home, that would have been fine. You know I would have loved having you close by. But none of them would do, as anyone with two thoughts to rub together could see. I mean, can you imagine, in your wildest dreams, being Mrs. Peter Abernathy?"

The three of them giggled, as they always did when Mrs. O'Connor said this. Peter Abernathy was a handsome young man, but he could barely count to ten.

"To give the boy credit, madam," said the maid, with the easy familiarity of an old family retainer, "he was smart enough to recognize what a gem our girl is."

"Quite right, Dolly. I should not malign the boy so," said Mrs. O'Connor.

Kate smiled as her mother and the maid laughed again. It was so good to hear her mother's laughter — it was pure and bright, like the water in a crystal clear brook. She studied her mother's face, watching for signs of fatigue. Her mother turned to gaze at her, giving her a reassuring wink.

"Here we are, Mrs. River's shop. When

we have finished with our fitting, dear, let's go to Gunter's for an ice."

"That would be wonderful," said Kate, hopping down and reaching back to help the maid descend. Together, they steadied her mother as she climbed down.

Two hours later, they had no thoughts of ices from Gunter's. There was that familiar tightness around her mother's eyes and mouth, and Kate insisted that she was too exhausted to go another step. The coachman turned the carriage toward their small house just off Berkley Square.

It was a modest residence, rented for the autumn Season. It suited their needs, having just enough room for the family and their few servants. Kate and Dolly helped Mrs. O'Connor to her room and saw her settled in the big bed. Her cheeks were the color of the white sheets, and Dolly declared that she would fetch a restorative.

"No, Dolly. That is not necessary. I only need to rest. I will be fine by dinner. Wake me when it is time to dress again."

"Very good, madam," said the maid, putting a finger to her lips as she led the way out of the room.

In the corridor, Kate motioned for the maid to follow her, and they went into her bedroom.

"She looks so very tired," said Kate, pitching her bonnet on the bed and peeling off her gloves. Dolly picked up the discarded items, checked them for loose ribbons or buttons, and then put them away.

"She'll be fine, miss. Your mother will come about. Just you wait and see. And when you start going to all those balls, she'll be right there with you." The maid returned to her young mistress's side and patted her head.

Kate managed a slight smile and said, "Sit down, Dolly, and tell me again about Mama's Season."

"Oh, miss, I've got a thousand things to do . . . oh, very well. Your mother was the prettiest belle of the Season, she was. She was tall and slender, like a reed. All the men were writing poems to her and making up the most dreadful songs."

"Did she receive flowers every day?"

"At least four or five bouquets every single day. And then there was that one day when among the bouquets there was a single daisy tied with a bright blue ribbon."

"From Papa," said Kate, who knew the story as well as the maid, but never tired of hearing about her mother and father's fairy-tale romance.

"Yes, and when your papa saw her wearing that ribbon that night, he knew she had chosen him. He was grinning from ear to ear, and your grandmama — rest her soul — she was fit to be tied. She tried to reason with your mama, but she would hear not a word against your papa. Your grandmama vowed she would not receive a penny of her dowry, but they refused to be swayed."

Kate sighed, marveling that her wealthy mother had chosen her penniless father over all her other suitors. That was how love was supposed to be, but she doubted that she would ever find such love. Perhaps she was too practical.

"I wonder what Papa will do if my choice displeases him," said Kate.

Dolly rose and grinned down at her mistress. "He will probably take the whip to him — and to you, too. Now stand up and let me help you out of that gown. I do not want to come back in here later and find it all wadded up on the bed."

It was midnight, much too late to be strolling outside in the tiny garden behind their rented house. Still, Kate was restless and needed to walk. Pulling her cloak around her nightrail, she shoved her feet into the half boots she had carried down to the kitchen and slipped outside.

It was quite dark, with only a sliver of moon peeking out from behind the clouds. Keeping to the wall of the house in case anyone should be looking out the windows, Kate made her way to the back of the walled garden and sat down on the cold stone bench. She gazed up at the stars that stubbornly shone through the thin clouds. Closing her eyes, she made her fervent wish: "I wish Mama would decide to let me go home again."

"What a deal of yearning to put in one short sentence," said a deep voice.

Kate leaped to her feet and whirled around.

"Who is there?" she demanded, more angry than afraid.

"Don't worry, little kitten, I mean you no harm. I'm your new neighbor, and I, too, was drawn outside by the stillness of the night."

Kate chuckled, relaxing at the cultured accents of the kindly voice.

"What is so funny?" he asked from behind the wall that separated his property from hers.

"It is obvious to me that you have yet to

see me if you call me little," she said.

"Oh? How intriguing. Perhaps I should climb . . ."

"No!" she said, pulling her cloak more tightly around her.

"What is wrong? I thought we had established that I do not mean you any harm," said the deep, velvety voice.

Kate grinned again. "Perhaps you do not, but I am not properly dressed underneath my cloak."

"All the more reason," he teased, but he made no move. "Shall I introduce myself?"

"If you like, though there can be nothing proper about such an introduction."

"No, I don't think I shall. I rather like speaking to a beautiful stranger in the night. It adds a certain piquancy to our conversation. One day we will meet properly. You will curtsy, and I will make a leg. Then you shall know my name. Until then, we will meet here, with the stars and the moon our candlelight."

"But how will we meet? We will not know each other in the daylight," said Kate.

"I would know you anywhere with that lovely lilting voice," claimed the gallant.

"Now you are being foolish," she chided.

"Dreams can make a man very foolish.

Perhaps it is the lateness of the hour, or the stars twinkling above."

"What shall I call you?"

"You may call me Sir Milton, and you shall be my Iseult."

"Then you should be Tristram."

"Real life is seldom like the legends, Iseult."

"Which you must admit is a very good thing in some cases, Sir Milton."

"I suppose you are right."

"I should go in before someone discovers us. I hope to hear from you again, Sir Milton. Good night."

"*Bonne nuit, ma petite,*" he said, and Kate hurried back to the house, her heart racing at the audacity of flirting with a man she neither knew nor could see.

When she was safe in her room again, she drew back the curtains, hoping to be able to see into the neighboring garden. She was out of luck. Several small trees obstructed her view, and she let the curtain fall.

"Stoopid," she murmured.

How foolish she was being, her heart fluttering over a man's silliness. She had always prided herself on her directness and had laughed at the other young ladies when they batted their eyes and sighed over some man. Now, she was doing the same — and all for a deep masculine voice that cascaded over the ears like velvet on the skin.

"Stoopid," she whispered again, climbing into bed and pulling up the counterpane.

Raising up on one elbow to blow out the lone candle on her nightstand, Kate smiled into the darkness. The first ball was on Sunday night. She had almost a week of midnights to hear that voice and his honeyed words.

Kate frowned. What if he did not return? But he had said he would, that they would meet again under the stars. If he did not return, she would have the measure of the man and count it as a small loss. But if he did return to the garden wall . . .

Kate rolled over and hugged her pillow. With a sweet smile, she fell asleep.

Two

Max rose early the next day in his pursuit of Thunderlight. While he knew he could not afford to buy the stallion, perhaps if he discovered who was riding him, he might figure something out. Surely that slip of a girl was not the owner! If only he had not lost her in the crowd the day before.

He was mounted on a big gray gelding, another of the Marquess of Cravenwell's horses. While Max was thankful that he had access to such excellent horseflesh while in London, he would have felt much better if only he could strangle the marquess for losing Thunderlight.

He rode through the park twice, but there was no sign of Thunderlight. Frustrated, he tried once more, but still had no luck. Dejected, he turned the big gelding back toward the stable.

As he neared the gates, the same black carriage that had almost hit him the day before entered the park. Max pulled back on the reins, his eyes widening in appreciation at the beauty on the seat gazing back at him, her hands clasped in her lap, her pretty straw bonnet tilted at a jaunty angle over blond curls. He tipped his hat and smiled. The girl lowered her eyes, but turned her head to look at him as the carriage passed by.

"Whew, that one is a rare beauty," he said, patting his horse's glossy mane. "Come on, let's go home. We're not going to find Thunderlight today."

Max spent the remainder of the day at Tattersall's, meeting friends and advising them on which horses they should select. His queries about an Irish horse breeder turned up a name, but no address, so he was no closer to finding Thunderlight.

From Tattersall's, he went to his club to meet more friends for dinner. It was a modest place with the august name of Regent's, which catered to the younger men with little money. It was little more than a coffee house, but it was a place where Max could be certain of enjoying a decent meal with a congenial group of friends. They urged him to join them for a night of revelry at one of Pall Mall's gaming hells, but Max had no interest in losing the small purse he was carrying.

The clock was striking midnight when he arrived home. Tristram, who was busily writing on his tome, merely waved a distracted hand to his greeting. Bored, Max accepted the glass of port Barton poured for him and wandered outside.

It was turning cooler, and he hunched his shoulders against the stiff breeze. Taking a pull on the drink, Max sat down on a stone bench, gasping as the cold penetrated his pantaloons. He swallowed wrong and began to cough.

"Sir Milton, are you all right?" asked a feminine voice.

Max jumped up and spun around. "Who's there?"

"It is I, Iseult. I heard you coughing. Are you all right?"

"Yes, I'm fine." He cleared his throat.

"You sound very different. Are you sure you're all right?"

"Yes, I'm sure. I . . . I beg your pardon, but what are you doing out here in the middle of the night?" Max grinned at the sound of her giggle. "I mean, I am delighted to find such an intriguing tenant in the garden next door, but surely you should be inside, away from the cold."

"I am not at all cold, Sir Milton, and I was hoping you would return tonight."

"Return . . . oh, I see," said Max, glancing at the house where his little brother was working so diligently. Tristram

was so wrapped up in his work, he must
have started something and then forgotten
all about the girl. Well, Max was more than
willing to carry on an anonymous flirtation
with such a captivating voice.

"Are you not afraid someone will discover our little assignation?" he asked, settling back on the bench and leaning
against the garden wall.

"No, everyone is asleep. Mama is . . . still
recovering from an indisposition, and Papa
prefers rising early to staying out late. That
is why Mama will have to be the one to accompany me to the balls and other entertainments."

"Oh, so Iseult is going to the balls."

"Yes, next Monday night."

"Your first ball," he said.

"Yes . . . I mean no. That is, it will be my
first in London. I have been to many
others, but not here."

"So, like all the other young ladies, you
have come to London to find a husband,"
said Max.

"Perhaps, but . . . never mind. I should
be going."

"No, stay," he whispered, turning to face
the wall.

"I . . . I should not," she replied.

He could hear the hesitation in her voice

and said, "But you will."

"Yes, a little longer."

"Good. Tell me, little Iseult, where are you from?"

She giggled. "As I told you last night, Sir Milton, you really must stop calling me little. I am all of five feet nine in my stocking feet."

"Ah, a statuesque beauty," he murmured.

"How . . . how tall are you?" she asked, her tone almost anxious.

"I am six feet tall — a mountain of a man, so they tell me."

"Oh, that is tall," she said breathlessly.

"Tall enough for a girl as magnificent as you," he added.

She gave a little gasp that made him laugh. He could tell from the height of her voice that, in her confusion, she must have leaped to her feet. He rose also.

"Will you leave me so soon?" he asked.

"I must go back inside. Good night, Sir Milton."

"Good night, fair Iseult."

Then he was alone. Max walked back to the house, a broad smile on his face. He rather thought he would enjoy living in the little house with its enchanting neighbor.

"Tristram, I just met the most interesting person."

41

"That's good," replied his brother, not bothering to look up. "Another one like you, who thinks horses are better than people?"

"Hm? As to that, I could not say. I shall have to ask her." Max waited to see if this comment would elicit more interest. When it did not, he wandered to his room and flopped down on the bed to while away the time, thinking of the beauty who most certainly belonged to that charming voice.

Almost as tall as he. That would be most interesting, he thought as he drifted off to sleep.

The remainder of the week, Max spent every morning in the park. He began to lose hope that he would see Thunderlight again, but he went anyway, and he always happened to be at the entrance at eleven o'clock to watch the beauty pass through the gates. She still lowered her eyes, but she smiled each time she saw him. He wished he could find the occasion to stop the carriage and introduce himself, but the dragon beside the girl scowled at him merely for looking. When there was a ball, then he would have the opportunity to meet her, to ask her to dance with him.

Twice he returned to the garden wall to

wait in vain for the mysterious Iseult to reappear. If she was a lady, she had probably come to her senses and realized how improper their midnight meeting had been. Max consoled himself with the thought that their neighbor was probably as plain as she was tall.

He much preferred the petite beauty in the park. She was just what he was looking for in a wife — shy, beautiful, and, he hoped, plump in the pocket. If she were only half as sweet as she was beautiful, then he might be willing to wed her.

It never occurred to Maxwell Darby that the girl might have very different ideas.

Saturday brought a cold wind whipping through the streets and warning London's occupants that winter was indeed on its way. It was the first week of October, and the wind brought with it Viscount Tavistoke, up from the country to urge his sons toward their objectives — finding wealthy wives.

When Barton opened the door to his knock, it flew out of his hands, banging forcefully against the wall. The viscount strode across the threshold, tearing off his gloves and throwing them to the surprised servant.

"Whom may I say . . . is . . . calling," huffed Barton, trailing after the viscount.

"Calling? I ain't calling. I'm here to see my boys." The viscount peered up at the servant and added, "You must be Barton. Cravenwell told me he had assigned you to the lads. Where are they? Ought to be up to greet their dear papa."

"If we had known you were coming, Papa, we would have been up," said Max, entering the room and fastening the frogs on his silk banyan.

"I will bring coffee, Master Max," said Barton, scurrying from the room.

"And where is Tristram?"

"Should be in bed, covering his head with his pillow if he has any sense at all," said Max. "Have a seat, Papa."

The viscount, who was already seated, glared at his son.

"Did you just arrive in town?"

"No, I got here last night. I'm staying with Cravenwell, you know. I don't think we would deal well together, the three of us, in this pokey little house."

"Oh? Do you find it pokey?" said Max, glancing around as if seeing the house for the first time. "I find it quite charming and spacious. Just the thing for me and Tris."

"Demme, boy. Have you no eyes? Hardly

bigger than those rooms you had last year. Besides, I've no desire to stay in a house where Cravenwell used to keep his mistresses."

"Ah, that would account for Tristram's pink bedchamber," said Max. "Speak of the devil. Good morning, Tris. Only see who has come to call."

"Not staying with us, are you, Papa?"

"Ungrateful wretch," growled his father. "No, I ain't. I'm with the marquess. You look like the devil."

"Why, thank you, Papa. As it happens, I was working until the wee hours of the morning."

"Were you? Good for you!" exclaimed the viscount. "Tell me, what is she like? Listen and learn, Maxwell. So what is she like? Rich? And beautiful, too, I'll be bound. The apple doesn't fall far from the tree. You would do well to take a page out of your little brother's book."

Max shouted with laughter, and Tristram twisted uncomfortably in his chair.

"Papa!" said Tristram.

"Papa, you have hit the nail on the head. The book you spoke of is just that. Our Tristram was up all night working on a book, a novel of epic proportions."

"Reading a book? All night? You're no son of mine," said the viscount, his nose scrunched up in distaste.

"Not reading, Papa," said his youngest son. "I am writing a book. My second book, if you must know. The first one will be out by the end of the week, or so my publisher tells me. He was merely waiting on the last few pages before printing and binding it."

"Your publisher? Bah! What sort of occupation is that for a gentleman? A gentleman is supposed to be a farmer, a gambler, a . . ."

"A fortune hunter?" added Max, the grin on his face making his brother and father scowl at him.

"There is nothing wrong with looking to your future when you are looking for a wife," said the viscount.

Barton entered with a tray and handed out coffee all around. Then he discreetly slipped out of the room.

"So how much are you being paid?" the viscount demanded.

"I would prefer to keep such information confidential," said Tristram.

"Humph! Then it ain't enough to amount to anything. You would do better to forget that silly book and concentrate on finding you a wife. I daresay Max already has someone in mind. Right, my boy?"

"I have met a couple of girls."

"There, you see? That is more like it. What are their names? I'll find out how deep their family pockets are."

"I'm afraid I don't know their names yet. Except for one. I know her first name. It is Iseult."

Tris swiveled to stare at his older brother.

"Iseult." The viscount drained his cup and rose. "Can't be too many fillies about with a name like that. I'll make inquiries. In the meanwhile, get busy . . . both of you!"

With this, he passed into the hall, and they heard the door slam against the wall again. Barton, who had been lingering close by, rushed to shut it against the terrible wind.

"Whew! Next time the wind is blowing like this, Barton, bolt the door and don't open it for anybody!" declared Max, rising and heading for his room.

"Max, where did you meet this Iseult?" asked Tristram.

"As if you don't know, Sir Milton. You are a sly one," he added.

"Not really. I had forgotten all about her."

"Tris, I hate to side with our father on this, but you really should get out of the house more. You're too wrapped up in those books of yours."

Tristram's brow rose in disdain. "You are a strange one to be giving me advice. You have been out almost constantly, but you have nothing more to show for your efforts than I do. Rather less, since I received a tidy little sum for my first book, the one I left with the publisher last spring."

"I didn't even realize you had written one. Congratulations, little brother. I am proud of you, but it still can't be as much as a hefty dowry."

"I know. And I will get out of the house," said Tristram, rising and going to the mantel where a small pile of invitations waited. Picking up the first one, he said, "Lady Murray's ball this Monday. We'll begin our campaigns in earnest then."

"Very good," said Max, wondering if this was the ball the mysterious Iseult was going to attend. Very likely. There could not be that many, not during the Little Season. "Tell me again, Tris, what is the name of the hero in your books?"

"Sir Milton."

"Is there a heroine?"

Tristram blushed and said, "Iseult."

Max grinned and nodded. "Monday it is!"

"I think it very badly done of Papa to deny me the right to visit the stables anymore," grumbled Kate. "I have been cooped up in this house for days on end!"

"Nonsense, my dear. We went to service just yesterday morning. And we have paid calls every afternoon."

"Yes, but that does not count. I want to go riding in the park by myself."

Her mother and their maid murmured sympathetically, but they were too busy studying her in the mirror to really pay attention to her words.

"I cannot like it," said Mrs. O'Connor. "To cut off all that glorious hair . . ."

"I promise you, madam, zee hair will be as beautiful as your daughter," said the tall, fussy man with scissors in his hands.

"Couldn't you just, oh, I don't know, tame it a little?"

The hairdresser sighed. "I do not see 'ow, madam. It is no more than a mop as it is. Where do I start?"

"I tell you where you start, Mr. Popinjay . . ."

"Now, Dolly, I'm sure Monsieur Poupin meant no insult," said Mrs. O'Connor.

49

"What do you think, Kate? It is your hair, after all."

"I am surprised anyone even noticed that little fact," she snapped.

"Miss Kate!"

"Oh, very well. I apologize, Mama, but I am so very aggravated. I really do not wish to cut my hair, but if it is the fashion, then I suppose it must be done."

The hairdresser held his scissors in readiness. Mrs. O'Connor stroked the long red curls and shuddered before giving a nod. The hairdresser set to his work with uncommon glee, whacking off long tresses before beginning to snip more judiciously, here and there.

Finally, he stood back, waving his scissors with a flourish.

"I give you, Miss O'Connor!"

Mrs. O'Connor and Dolly stepped forward, looking at Kate's face in the glass, framed by clusters of red curls.

"Oh, you do look a treat, Miss Kate," breathed the maid.

Mrs. O'Connor smiled at her daughter and nodded in approval. Kate returned the smile.

"Do you like it, dear?"

"It is quite different, but yes, I do like it."

"Of course she likes it!" declared the hairdresser. "It is perfect for her face, perfect for her hair. No one else would dare to cut her hair so short, but me, I know what is best. You see how it makes her neck look swan-like. Yes this, this is my masterpiece! Other girls will beg me to do the same for them, but I will say no! This," he said, taking Kate's chin and turning her head from side to side, "this is only for Miss O'Connor, because only she can handle such an extraordinary masterpiece!"

"Thank you, Mr. Poupin," said Kate, who felt like giggling. Looking at her image, for the first time in her life she felt beautiful. As far as she was concerned, Mr. Poupin's work was more miracle than masterpiece.

"Yes, thank you, Monsieur Poupin. Now, Kate, do rest for an hour. I will send Dolly to you to help you dress for the ball," said her mother, kissing her on top of the head before shooing everyone from the room.

After running the comb through her hair and twice scratching her swan-like neck, Kate rose and went to the bed, stretching out across it and closing her eyes. Turning this way and that, she found sleep was impossible. She was about to go to her first

51

London ball, and she was ridiculously nervous.

She couldn't imagine why. She was five and twenty and had attended countless balls and danced with all sorts of men. Why she should suddenly be nervous, she could not understand. She had met many people since arriving in London, and she had felt no shyness with them. What was more, it was her aunt's ball, so she should certainly feel at home.

Kate gazed at the Pomona green gown hanging on the front of the wardrobe. The color was as fresh as spring, and the cut was simple. It had long, fitted sleeves and a deep decolletage to show off her ample charms. Her aunt, Lady Murray, had sent over an emerald pendant on a short ribbon. When she had held it up to her throat, her father had said proudly that it matched her sparkling green eyes perfectly.

Everything was ideal, so why had butterflies taken up permanent residence in her stomach? Surely it could not be because she was to meet Sir Milton. She had waited for the household to grow quiet each night, but her father had taken to inviting his cronies over to play cards every night, which meant the servants, too, were keeping late hours. Kate had not judged it safe to venture outside again.

She had begged the cook and their footman to find out more about their neighbor, but they knew nothing. When all was said and done, it was all a hum, anyway. The man next door was probably most unsuitable and nothing out of the ordinary when seen in the daylight. He was probably five inches shorter than she was and as wide as he was tall. Even if he had managed to secure an invitation to her aunt's ball, she would probably not look twice at him.

If, on the other hand, he were as tall and charming as his voice and words . . . there went those butterflies again.

The key to being all the kick in London Society was to be unique, but not too unique. With Monsieur Poupin's newly styled hair, Kate O'Connor managed to walk that fine line. She was worldly enough to realize, of course, that by the next ball, her looks might be considered passé. But for this night, it amused and pleased her that her short red curls were the talk of her aunt's ballroom.

Upon entering the ballroom, Kate stopped to gaze down at the bright colors of the ladies' gowns as the couples went through the motions of the dance. The butterflies took flight again. One of those men might be Sir Milton. 'Twas not his real name, she felt sure, but she would use it to help identify him — if she were lucky enough to hear his voice and if he was in attendance. She told herself once again not to set her hopes too high.

"Come along, my dear. There is Lady Nance with her handsome grandson. Her son was one of my suitors all those years ago. He was just as handsome as this young man. I will introduce you." Obediently, Kate followed her mother.

"I will meet up with you two later," called her father, turning and heading toward his brother-in-law's study, where he knew Lord Murray would be hiding with a few old friends, playing at whist or hazard.

As she and her mother neared the young man and elderly matron, Kate whispered, "He is not very tall."

"No, but he is quite suitable in every other way. We talked about that. The perfect man is not always as tall as you are," said her sensible mother.

"No, but Sir Milton is," muttered Kate before pasting on her smile for the introduction. Before Kate could spare another thought for the shadowy Sir Milton, she was swept into the forming set by Lord Nance.

"How do you find London, Miss O'Connor?" he asked politely before they were separated by the steps of the dance.

"It is charming, my lord."

"So have you seen all the sights, visited all the exhibits? Or perhaps you are like most young ladies, and the shops have taken all your time."

They were separated by the movements, and Kate was able to compose herself before responding. She wondered what his reaction would be if she told him she preferred mucking out a stall to shopping for ribbons and such.

"So have you managed to empty the shops like my sister has? I can tell that you have found a talented modiste, because the gown you are wearing is both fashionable and very becoming," said Lord Nance, dragging his eyes away from her decolletage and smiling at her.

"I have purchased one or two things, my lord, though I am not allowed inside the one place where I truly wish to go."

They separated again, and Kate wanted to laugh at his expression while he tried to imagine which forbidden spot she was talking about.

"What place is that?" he asked quickly when they again met and began a promenade in the circle.

"Tattersall's, my lord. I simply adore Tattersall's, but my father refuses to let me go there. Do you not think that is cruel of him?"

"No. That is, I am sure he . . . well, Tattersall's is not the proper place for a young lady. I cannot fathom why you wish to go there."

"Horses are my passion, Mr. Nance, and I often help my father select his horses. We were fortunate enough to secure an excellent stallion recently, but we could use some more brood mares for him. New blood is essential in the horse breeding game, you know."

The music ended, and Lord Nance hurried her back to her mother. Mrs. O'Connor frowned over his haste, but she was prevented from questioning Kate since she had two young men waiting to ask her daughter for the next dance.

She went from Lord Nance to Mr. Haynes and so on, dancing the night away. While Kate's frank conversation shocked some of her partners, others were fascinated by her candor and asked for second dances. These men, Kate decided, would need further discouragement. They were entirely too persistent. If she was going to be able to return home to Ireland, she would have to send them packing.

Kate's other objective was more private. She had avoided examining her motives too closely on why she wanted to find the shadowy Sir Milton. If marrying did not fit in with her plans, then why was she so set on meeting him face to face? Still, as she moved around the ballroom with her partners, Kate searched for a "mountain of a man" among the other dancers. And she listened — listened for that deep, appealing voice.

The musicians took a break around two o'clock, and the butler announced grandly that a supper buffet awaited them in the dining hall. Kate, who had just completed a waltz with a Mr. Osgood, shrugged away from him, claiming that she had torn her flounce. Not waiting for him to notice that her green gown did not boast a flounce, she hurried away.

Her butterflies had long since fled. After all, there was no reason for anxious anticipation when it was quite obvious that Sir Milton was not at her aunt's ball. Probably he had never been invited. She harbored a keen sense of disappointment and couldn't understand why.

She did not wish to marry, did not wish to live in crowded London where a lady had to abide by so many silly rules: No riding without a groom. No galloping in the park. No moonlight trysts in the garden.

Kate bit back a frustrated groan.

"I simply don't have time for all this, Papa. I have to get back to my manuscript."

Kate stopped in her tracks, forgetting to turn the handle as she pressed on the door to the ladies' withdrawing room. When it did not open, she bumped her nose, but she didn't care.

It was him! It had to be his voice on the other side of the potted plant that had been placed to screen the entrance to the ladies' room. Stealthily, Kate inched closer and pushed a branch to one side to get a better view.

"My boy, you will never succeed if you leave every ball this early," said a short, balding man in elegant evening dress, the one her Sir Milton had addressed as Papa.

"I told you they didn't have what it takes, Tavistoke," said another man, whom she recognized as the Marquess of Cravenwell. Her aunt had pointed him out earlier, calling him the dirty marquess.

Over the head of the father, Kate saw him, her Sir Milton. He was tall, broad-shouldered, and blond. Hmm, she had pictured him dark. He seemed to be looking right at her, and she let the branch fall, taking a step back.

"I have to agree with Papa on this, Tristram. It is rude to leave before dinner."

It was another voice, one similar, but not her Sir Milton . . . at least, she did not think it was he. Their voices were so very similar. Perhaps she was mistaken.

Cautiously, she lifted the branch and peered through the plant again to discover what sort of man this second voice belonged to. This one was just as tall, but dark. His back was to her, and she could not see his face.

The tall blond, the one called Tristram, finally capitulated, saying, "Oh, very well. I will remain, but I am excusing myself immediately after this dashed supper. This is only the first ball."

"First or last, you are wasting both my time and my money if you leave before supper. That's when all the hand-holding and flirtation really begin, and don't you forget it," said the dirty marquess.

"What's more . . . oh, blast!" exclaimed the father of the two handsome men.

A trill of feminine laughter severed their intimate conversation, and Kate smiled as a purple-turbaned dame came sailing toward the men. Ignoring the other three, she zeroed in on the young men's father.

"La, there you are, Tavistoke. I vow, I have searched the entire house for you, naughty man. You told me you were going to lead me into supper. Now, come along."

Without further ado, she linked arms with the hapless man and led him away.

The Marquess of Cravenwell took a step to follow. Then, turning to face the two younger men, he said, "From the looks of things, that father of yours may make it to the altar before either of you do. But you just remember, I will have my pound of flesh, one way or the other."

With this, the marquess stalked away, leaving the two younger men behind.

"I wish Papa and Cravenwell had not come tonight," said the blond. "It is going to be very annoying, having them always looking over our shoulders."

"Yes, but perhaps Papa has found someone else to occupy his time. Do you know who that was? Lady Anne Graves," said the dark-haired man. When the blond showed no interest in this information, he said sharply, "Lady Anne is only the richest spinster in England."

Tristram laughed and said, "I only hope she will keep Papa occupied so that he will not bother us."

"Chin up, Tris. Things could be worse. Papa could be staying with us instead of at Cravenwell's house. Now, come along to supper. I want to show you the prettiest girl at the ball."

The younger man brightened and asked, "Have you found the mystery lady from the garden?"

"No, how would I know her? I haven't even thought of her. No, I'm talking about the blond beauty from the park. Do you never listen to anything I say?"

Kate stepped back, almost falling through the door to the ladies' withdrawing room as an abigail opened it.

"Excuse me, miss. Did you need some help?"

"What? Oh, no thank you. I am fine," she said, closing the door in the maid's face. She needed time to think.

Max hurried toward the supper room, his long stride matched by his brother.

"What does this beauty look like?" asked Tristram.

"You'll see."

"You haven't actually been presented to her yet, have you?"

"No, but I did find out her name. It is Philippa Beauchamp. Have you ever heard a lovelier name? Look, there she is. That bore, Osgood, is serving her. How the devil did that happen? Palmer was the one who led her out in the supper dance."

"What does it matter? No, there's Palmer, talking to that . . . I was about to say lightskirt, but that is hardly likely here."

"Who cares? I know Palmer, and that is enough to secure an introduction. Come on. It won't be so obvious with the two of us choosing to sit at their table."

Tristram tagged along obediently.

"Palmer, how good to see you."

"Darby, I didn't know you had gotten back into town. Understand you have lost that stallion of yours," said Palmer, a slight sneer on his face.

"While I was away, I'm afraid," said Max, reaching behind him and pulling his brother forward. "You remember Tristram, do you not?"

"Darby, good to see you, both of you. Won't you join us?"

Max made a show of looking around for another table before pulling up a chair and beckoning Tristram to do the same.

"Allow me to present Mrs. Beauchamp and her lovely daughter, Miss Philippa Beauchamp. This is Mr. Max Darby and his brother Tristram."

Max was lost in the biggest, bluest eyes he had ever seen. Smiling, he gave a nod of his head to the beauty, but he could not manage to speak.

"Now, Mr. Palmer, there is no harm in being truthful, is there? You need not play the shy gentleman with me. I would never hold it against you if should you introduce us as the lovely Mrs. Beauchamp and her daughter. You needn't play on my sympathies by complimenting my little girl. And a child she is, don't you know, gentlemen? Not to say one cannot be wed at her age. I was her mother by the time I was her tender years. A child bride, they called me."

The table fell silent while Mrs. Beauchamp's amazed listeners digested her words. All at once, the gentlemen realized that a compliment had been called for, and they rushed to comply.

"Of course, Mrs. Beauchamp, it is easy to see that Miss Beauchamp is a striking copy of her mother," said Palmer.

Osgood piped in, "A shadowy copy."

"Indeed, I thought you were sisters," said Max, who had guessed that his access to the daughter depended on his flattering the mother.

"Sisters? You must be . . ." Tristram fell silent beneath the others' shocked expressions. He clamped his lips together in mulish defiance.

"We are delighted to meet both of you charming ladies," said Max, trying to cover his brother's faux pas.

"You are too kind," said the matron, leaning forward and pursing her lips at him. "Looking at the two of you, I can hardly credit that you are brothers. You look nothing alike."

"We are both quite tall," said Max, smiling at the daughter.

"But you are dark and . . . well, I know you will not mind my candor, you are such a fine figure of a man. Your *little* brother, however, is blond and — ah, but then I suppose he will fill out nicely when he is grown. Dear me, I seem to have upset my plate," said the matron.

Mr. Osgood leaped to his feet, the contents of the overturned plate slipping off his lap.

"I am dreadfully sorry, Mr. Osgood. How clumsy of me. You go and get cleaned up. I'm sure Mr. Darby, Mr. Max Darby, will accompany me to the tables for a new plate."

As Mrs. Beauchamp rose, she managed to knock over her glass and said, "Oh, Mr. Palmer, not you, too. All that lovely champagne. Oh, dear. Philippa, my sweet, why don't you keep Mr. Tristram company while Mr. Max Darby and I take care of refilling my plate?"

"Yes, Mama."

Max offered his arm to the boorish mother, managing the smallest of smiles as he led her back to the buffet tables.

As he left, he heard Tristram say, "I am glad the plate did not soil your lovely gown, Miss Beauchamp."

"No, it does not usually do so," she replied before ducking her head shyly.

"I beg your pardon?"

She glanced up at him through her long lashes and smiled. "I should not have spoken. It is just Mama's way of ridding herself of gentlemen who have begun to bore her."

"I shall hope I never fall into that category," murmured Tristram.

"Oh, no, Mr. Darby. You would never . . ." The girl blushed a rosy pink and failed to finish her statement.

Smiling, Tristram said, "I think I saw you in the park the day we arrived in town."

"Yes, I thought that was you," whispered the girl.

"My brother has seen you several times. It was he who wanted so badly to meet you tonight."

"Really? And you?"

"Well, I had forgotten . . . that is, I have been very busy since we arrived in town. As for myself, I prefer . . . quieter pursuits."

"What sort of pursuits, Mr. Darby?"

"Oh, drawing, reading. Nothing as exciting as my brother," said Tristram.

"I like to draw, too, but I have very little talent," said the girl, still looking at her plate.

"You might be very surprised. Perhaps you would show them to me sometime."

"I would be too embarrassed," she whispered.

"Nonsense. If you never show them to anyone, how will you improve? I taught a young man back home . . ."

"You teach drawing?" she breathed, gazing up at him as if he had hung the moon. "Do you think . . . I mean, I would be honored if you would help me. I have the most difficult time with noses."

"Noses are not so difficult when you learn a trick or two. I would be happy to teach you. I mean, if we have the chance to meet again."

"But we must," she replied. "I . . . oh, here they come. Perhaps we will have another opportunity to speak of this?"

"Of course we shall. I know that my brother wants to get to know you better. He's a capital fellow."

"Yes, I'm sure he is," she whispered, falling silent as her overbearing mother and Max returned.

Kate spent the remainder of the night looking around the ballroom for her Sir Milton. It tickled her that his real name was Tristram. In the garden, he had called her his Iseult. Did that mean he thought they were destined to be together?

It was nonsense, of course, but it kept her mind occupied while her feet followed the movements of various dances. She smiled and murmured polite replies to her partners, but in her distracted state, that was the best she could manage.

After supper was over and two sets had passed, he was gone. She looked for him in vain. His dark-haired brother remained, but Tristram, her Sir Milton, was gone, and so was the sparkle in her green eyes.

The next time Kate returned to her mother, she said, "You look weary, Mama. May we go home?"

"Are you tired of dancing so soon? Why, during my Season, I danced till dawn every night."

"I am sure you did," said Kate with a weary smile. "However, I am not you, so may we go?"

"No one has said anything untoward to you, have they?" her mother asked anxiously. "I could not bear it if anyone maligned you because of me."

"Please believe that no one has said anything untoward about you or Papa. And why should they? When has being poor been more important than bloodline? We have nothing to be ashamed of," said Kate proudly.

"Oh, I know. I am just being silly. Perhaps I am more fatigued than I care to admit. Very well, I shall send for your father."

On the ride home, Kate's mind remained firmly fixed on the intriguing Tristram. She resolved to meet her neighbor face to face as quickly as possible. If there was one man in all of London who might convince her to give up her home and marry, it was Sir Milton. She had never heard her heart beat in such a irregular manner, like the silly schoolgirls said it did — never until this night.

Perhaps five and twenty was not too old for true love after all.

Three

Max paid a formal call on Miss Beauchamp and her mother the next day. He tried to persuade Tristram to accompany him, but his brother had had his fill of Mrs. Beauchamp at the ball. Mrs. Beauchamp had several gentlemen in attendance, but they did not seem overly interested in her daughter, preferring the mother's company to the daughter's, or so it seemed to Max.

Palmer and Osgood were there, and once again, Mrs. Beauchamp ignored them in favor of her latest acquisition, Maxwell Darby. She giggled, she rapped his arm with her fan, she flirted for all she was worth until finally Mrs. Beauchamp was ignoring everyone in favor of Max.

He glanced at Miss Beauchamp from time to time, but she never lifted her beautiful eyes.

After the requisite thirty minutes, Max resisted Mrs. Beauchamp's insistence that she needed him to remain longer and left.

The next day, Max sent some lace handkerchiefs, folded into the shape of a heart. Though he did not know it, these were appropriated by the mother.

After almost a week, Max felt he was making progress with the mother, which was what he needed to do, according to everyone who knew the family. Though he could not discover what scandal Mrs. Beauchamp had embroiled herself in the previous spring, he assumed it had something to do with a man, perhaps even a lover.

As distasteful as Max found the mother, he was intrigued by the daughter. He could not believe she was as retiring as she acted. How could she be, with a mother like she had?

"What do you mean, she's gone?" said Mr. O'Connor the next morning, glaring at his head groom. "I left strict orders that she was not to go riding in the mornings. You know what she does, riding like the hounds of hell are nipping at her heels. Why did you let her go?"

MacAfee cocked one bushy brow and said tartly, "And how do you think I should go about stoppin' Miss Kate, sir? If you cannot stop her, what makes you think I can? If the young mistress tells me she's goin' for a ride on that stallion, who am I to tell her no? It would be naught but a waste of breath."

Kieran O'Connor snorted and sat down on a barrel, saying, "It's a cryin' shame that she is too old to turn over my knee."

"Ah, those were the days," said MacAfee, leaning against the doorsill of the tack room.

"How long has she been gone?"

"An hour. She did take the boy along, though he'll never keep up wi' her if she runs the beast."

"If?" said O'Connor, pulling a flask out of his pocket and taking a long pull. He offered it to the groom, who did the same before returning it.

"You and your missus, you have only boys, do you not?"

"Aye, and glad I am of it. Not but what Miss Kate isn't a fine young lady, because she is. Why, she's practically like a daughter to me. Still, it's a terrible responsibility, raising a girl," said the groom.

"It's demmed expensive, is what it is. Two of my best horses, and now Kate's mare. That's what these two months in London are costing me. A fortune." Shaking his head dolefully, he took another swig of the fiery liquid.

"Well, ye' did win that stallion. And I'm sure Miss Kate will find her a nice fellow here in London." MacAfee took another drink, too.

"I hope so, and what's more important, it's what her mother wants. Heaven help me, but I'll miss her," said O'Connor, taking another sip. He dashed a tear from his eye and rose. "Send her to me when she returns."

"That I will, sir."

Dressed in a bottle green habit, Kate kept the stallion at a trot as they entered the park. Her groom was at their heels until they reached the trees. Hidden from any casual passerby, Kate let out the reins, and Thunderlight broke into a canter. Ever mindful of her father's strictures, she kept him at this sedate pace for the next few minutes. The big horse shook his head in protest, but he was well mannered enough to obey.

"Sorry, big fellow, but not today. When we get home to Ireland, then I'll let you have your head. You're going to love it there." She twisted in the saddle to see if her young groom had caught up with them yet.

"Hey! Hey, you! Wait, miss! Wait!"

As she turned around again, Kate frowned at the approaching horseman.

There was something familiar . . . ah, yes, she thought. It was Tristram's brother. At the thought of Tristram, her heart did another of those strange flips. She pulled the restive stallion to a halt and waited for the dark-haired man's approach.

"Good morning, miss," he said, giving her a nod.

Her nose slightly elevated to show that she was not in the habit of conversing with just any strange gentleman who hailed her, she said, "Good morning, sir. I'm sorry. Have we met?" Never mind that he was her neighbor. He couldn't know that she and his brother had twice conversed in the garden at midnight — twice.

"No, not formally. My name is Maxwell Darby. I saw you one day in the park last week, though I daresay you did not notice me as you flew past." He leaned forward and touched Thunderlight's nose. The stallion gave a gentle snort and shook his head. The man smiled and said, "As a matter of fact, I have been searching for you ever since that day."

"Really? What on earth for?"

"Because you have my horse!"

"Because . . . I beg your pardon! This horse belongs to me — or, rather, to my father."

74

"No, no, I don't mean my horse. I mean, oh, devil take me. I've started this all wrong."

"I think you have, sir. Good day to you." Kate turned the stallion toward the gates. The sooner she got away from this man the better. He might be her Sir Milton's brother, but he was all about in the head if he thought her horse belonged to him!

A sharp whistle sounded, causing her to jump. Thunderlight stopped, refusing to budge. Another long whistle and the stallion reared up and pivoted. Kate held on for dear life as his feet pounded the ground, and he trotted back toward her neighbor. Shaken, Kate tried to turn the horse, but he was determined.

"Hallo, Thunderlight," said Mr. Darby, scratching behind the stallion's ears as the big horse butted his head against the man's chest. "Sorry, but I couldn't let you get away again. May I start over?"

"Please do," said Kate, her lips pursed and her eyes narrowing angrily. It was a rare happening when she could not control her horse, and she did not like it or this brother of her Sir Milton, not one bit!

"I know that your father won Thunderlight in a fair match race. What I should have said was that I . . . what I meant was, when I am in town, the Marquess of Cravenwell allows me the run of his stables. Last spring, it was I racing Thunderlight, and winning every time, I might add. He's a magnificent horse."

Thawing slightly, Kate smiled and patted the stallion's neck. "Yes, he is wonderful. But I don't understand. What happened?"

"I went home to the country for the summer, but the marquess, I suppose, enjoyed winning those races. He continued to race him, but with his groom riding Thunderlight. That was his big mistake. If I had been riding him, he never would have lost to your father."

"Really?" said Kate, looking him up and down. "I take leave to doubt that, sir. You must weigh half again as much as that groom. And since I was the one on our gelding that morning . . . oh, I should not have said that. Papa told me not to tell anyone. Please, Mr. Darby, you will keep that to yourself, will you not?"

"On one condition — Miss O'Connor, isn't it?"

She nodded, but she asked warily, "Kate O'Connor. How did you know that?"

"I made inquiries about the race and Thunderlight. I found out a man named O'Connor won the stallion, but I could not discover his direction," said Max.

"I see," said Kate, studying his face and thinking how very handsome he was. He cleared his throat, and she said, "You spoke of a condition, Mr. Darby?"

With a winning smile, he continued, "Yes, it is that you allow me to ride Thunderlight one last time."

"No, I cannot. I should not."

"I promise you, I only want a moment or two."

Those deep blue eyes gazing soulfully into hers won her over, and she said, "Oh, very well. I suppose no harm can come of letting you put him through his paces."

He slid off his gray gelding and held up his hands to help her dismount. Kate rolled her eyes and motioned him away. She had no need of help when it came to horses, and she was impatient with any man who thought otherwise.

A moment later, her sidesaddle lay on the ground, and Mr. Darby swung onto the big stallion's back. Kate held the big gray and watched as Thunderlight pranced across the grass, practically dancing while Max Darby guided him this way and that. He bent over the stallion's glossy neck, speaking to the stallion. Thunderlight grew still, listening and waiting. Suddenly, Mr.

Darby gave him the office to start, and they flew across the park and out of sight.

Kate waited a moment, consoling herself with the fact that she had the advantage of knowing Mr. Darby was her neighbor and would be easy to find when she had him arrested for a horse thief.

The groom, who had been watching all this in silence, said sorrowfully, "Mr. MacAfee's goin' to boil me in oil, he is."

"Nonsense, Bobby. They will be back in a moment."

It was closer to five minutes before Thunderlight and Mr. Darby appeared at the far end of the clearing. Kate heaved a sigh of relief.

Her eyes sparkled as she watched the pair. Thunderlight was dancing once again, as if overjoyed to have Mr. Darby riding him. If ever she had seen a horse and rider who belonged together, it was these two.

Mr. Darby slid to the ground and handed the reins to her groom. With quiet expertise, her handsome neighbor switched the saddles. Turning, he cupped his hands to throw her into the saddle. Then, with a final pat, he swung up on his gray gelding.

"Thank you, Miss O'Connor. I enjoyed that. I wish . . . thank you."

He turned his horse around, but stopped when Kate said quietly, "If I can get away, Mr. Darby, I am usually in this area of the park by ten o'clock each morning. If you would care to ride with us."

His smile transformed his face, and he nodded, lifting his hand in salute before trotting away.

Kate watched him until he was out of sight. He might not be her Sir Milton, but Max Darby was a very handsome man. She suspected that he had caused more than a few hearts to flutter.

"We should be getting back, miss."

"What? Oh, yes. Let's go. And, Bobby, I don't think we need mention this to my father or to Mr. MacAfee."

"Bless you, Miss Kate."

"I have found him!" exclaimed Max, throwing open the drawing room door, causing his brother to break the point on his pen.

"Found who?" said Tristram, picking up the knife to trim the point yet again.

"Thunderlight, of course!"

Tris put down his pen and turned around to face his older brother. "Where was he? Who has him?"

"I saw the same girl riding him in the

park again, although she was not racing across the grass. She actually had him under control enough to keep him at a canter. I watched her for several minutes before showing myself. I was afraid to wait any longer because I thought she would give him his head, or lose control, at any minute."

"But who is it?"

"It's like I told you before. It's a Miss O'Connor. Her father is the Irish horse breeder I told you about. Blast!"

"What is it?"

"I forgot to ask where they are staying. Little good it has done me to know the man's name, since no one seems to know where they live."

"I'm surprised that you would forget that."

"Well, it's understandable. I was so excited to ride Thunderlight again . . ."

"She let you ride him?"

"Oh, yes. What's more, she told me she would be at the park tomorrow morning, if I should wish to join her. I tell you, Tris, she is an unusual girl. Not beautiful, not like Miss Beauchamp, but she possesses something indefinable. And her hair? Bright red, and short — most unusual and attractive."

"Oh-ho!" said Tristram, raising an eyebrow.

"No, no, I am completely committed to Miss Beauchamp, especially since the marquess said her family is both wealthy and desperate."

"I did not understand that," said Tristram. "Why would they be desperate when Miss Beauchamp is such a beauty? And so very sweet. I am sure you could not find a more agreeable creature. Surely she will have suitors galore."

"She may be all that you say, but according to Cravenwell, the mother is the problem. She scares them away, trying to flirt with them herself. She also got into some sort of scandal last year. The whole family had to go and rusticate in the country until everything blew over."

"Despicable. No wonder Miss Beauchamp is quiet as a mouse. She is probably ashamed of her mother's antics."

"Yes, well, you leave the mother to me. I have accepted the mother's invitation for both of us to go for a drive along Rotten Row this afternoon."

"Us? I don't want to be anywhere near that woman! She frightened me half to death last night!"

"Yes, I could see it in your eyes. I would

have laughed, but I was too busy ingratiating myself with the dreadful woman. Don't worry. I'll be doing the same thing this afternoon. All you have to do is talk to Miss Beauchamp and tell her what a capital chap I am, how much I admire her, and so on. You can handle that, can you not?"

"I suppose so, but I would much rather be forced to ride that stallion of yours than to spend five minutes trapped in a carriage with that pushy female."

"Whew, you really were put off by her! I have never heard you say you would rather be on horseback."

"Exactly," said Tristram, turning back to his manuscript, picking up his pen, and dipping it in the pot of ink.

"But you'll be ready to go at half past four, will you not?" said Max.

"I'll be ready," grumbled his brother.

Max grinned and went out the back door, whistling softly as he traversed the garden and sat down on the small bench near the wall. Feeling rather foolish, he nevertheless called quietly, "Iseult! Iseult!"

"Stoopid," he said, leaning back and closing his eyes.

It had felt great to be up on Thunderlight again. He was glad he had taught him to answer that whistle. Otherwise, the girl might have ridden away, and he would never have seen the big stallion again — or the girl.

Max frowned. He was obviously very taken by that girl to have mentioned her to Tristram in such glowing terms and then to think of her again. She was only the daughter of an Irish horse breeder, and she was hardly a great beauty.

Oh, but on horseback, she was magnificent. If he were the poetic sort — which he most certainly was not — he might even say that the girl and Thunderlight were like a work of art or bit of poetry. They moved so well together. At least Thunderlight's new owner would take care of him. The stallion loved to run so. He needed someone who would appreciate that, appreciate him, and he rather thought Miss O'Connor would do so.

There he was again, thinking of the girl instead of the horse. The daughter of an Irish horse breeder. He wondered if she would enjoy a bit of dalliance?

"No, no, no!" he muttered. He was supposed to be concentrating on the beautiful, sweet Miss Beauchamp. He would have to forget all about Miss O'Connor.

"Sir Milton? Is that you?" The furtive

whisper brought him to his feet.

"Yes, it is I, fair Iseult. I had lost hope of hearing your voice again."

"I . . . I cannot stay long, but I wanted to tell you that we should meet. Not more than an hour ago I . . . I met your brother in the park."

Max frowned. His brother? What the devil . . . Tristram hadn't been in the park. He had been the one . . .

He began to laugh, the sound growing until she began to shush him. "Sh! Someone will hear and wonder why I am talking to a wall, a laughing wall."

"I am sorry, fair Iseult. I had no idea . . ."

"No, of course you did not. It was your brother I met, but I think we should meet, too, face to face."

"Oh, I heartily agree, fair maiden," said Max, his amusement threatening to burst forth again. How ironic that he had spent the past week searching London for the mysterious Irish horse breeder and all the while he and his intriguing daughter lived right next door.

"Good. Your brother Max is to meet me tomorrow morning in Green Park. He knows where. Will you accompany him?"

"I shall count the hours, my dear Iseult."

"Until tomorrow morning," she whispered, and he could tell from her tone that she was smiling.

Then she was gone, leaving Max to chuckle to himself, marveling at his good fortune. Perhaps he should have been a gambler like his father — except that he would be lucky.

How fortuitous this visit to London was turning out to be. He had settled on a girl suitable to marry. Fortunately, her wealthy family wanted to see her settled quickly, so they would not quibble at his lack of fortune. In addition, he had discovered he was neighbor to a delightful scamp of a girl, who, if he played his cards right, might end up in his bed for a bit of fun before settling down to dull, married life.

Sometimes the fates did smile on him!

With her first ball under her belt, her mother's worries had eased, and Kate found she had more freedom again. It was not like at home in Ireland, but when she mentioned that she wanted to go shopping with only Dolly for company, her mother had not quibbled over the proposed expedition, only mentioning that she had promised to drive in the park with her and her aunt at five o'clock.

Their first stop took them to Layton and

Shears, the drapers on Henrietta Street, for some new ribbons to refurbish the gown she had worn the previous evening. Her mother insisted that Kate must do something to make it appear different, or she would be considered sadly out of fashion. She debated on blue or ivory, and finally chose the blue.

From there, they went to Nicholay's Fur and Feather Manufactory to purchase two ostrich plumes for one of her mother's headdresses. Finally, they arrived at Hatchards, number 187 Piccadilly, for the latest novels.

Dolly sat on a bench by the front door while Kate perused the shelves. She selected two novels and took them to the clerk at the front desk. The young man sat on his tall stool, his nose in a book, oblivious to everything around him. Kate cleared her throat. Finally, she tapped the counter, and the young man jumped.

"Oh, I beg your pardon, miss!" he exclaimed, his voice squeaking and his face turning red.

"That's all right," she replied, smiling at him. "You were so engrossed, I hated to disturb you."

"Oh, please, miss, you will not tell Mr. Goforth, will you?"

"Certainly not. I am no tattler," she replied. Then, picking up the book he had put down, she asked, "What are you reading that made you forget where you were?"

"It . . . it is a new novel, by someone named Mr. Poorman."

"I don't think I have heard of it before. Might I like it?"

"Oh, I don't know, miss. It's not like these two that you have selected. It is all about knights and adventures. There is only one girl in it."

"But the tale is well written?" asked Kate.

"Yes, miss. One of the best I have read yet."

"Do you have another copy of it? For I would not wish to purchase this one and deprive you of the pleasure of finishing it."

"Yes, miss, I have another right here. And these two?"

"Yes, please," said Kate, opening her reticule. Books were one of the luxuries she allowed herself. She often spent the evening reading to her mother, with Dolly nearby drinking in every word. This Mr. Poorman's novel might not appeal to her delicate mother, but it certainly did to her.

When Kate and Dolly arrived home, she

went straight to her room. Not bothering to change, she opened the novel. The very first line grabbed her interest as she read, " 'We will take the castle and save the damsel, even if she does not wish to be saved!' said Sir Milton."

Her excitement mounting, Kate began to read, her breath catching in her throat when the damsel turned out to be named Iseult. Almost panting, she frowned and set the book aside. Coincidence? How likely was it that her neighbor, the average Mr. Tristram Darby, would have chosen to call himself Sir Milton and to call her Iseult? It was impossible! thought Kate, picking up the book again. As incredible as it seemed, Tristram Darby had to be the author of this novel. She read another page and then smiled. Her Mr. Darby of the garden wall had a great deal more depth to him than she had previously guessed.

The smile still playing on her lips, Kate quickly lost herself in the story. She looked up in surprise when the clock chimed half past four. Reluctantly, she set the book aside and hurried to dress for her drive in the park with her mother and aunt.

"How do I look? Is my cravat . . ."
"Your cravat is fine," said Tristram, grin-

ning at his older brother and shaking his head. "Really, Max, the way you are behaving, one would never guess that you were as experienced with the ladies as you are."

"Experienced with other ladies is one thing, Tris. This is the one who counts," said Max, running a distracted hand through his hair.

"She must be quite taken with you. I mean, to invite us to join them in their carriage. That is rather telling, don't you think?"

"I don't know. It was Mrs. Beauchamp who extended the invitation," said Max. "I must say, it is rather difficult to tell if I am making any headway or not. I have no experience with courting someone like Miss Beauchamp, where the mother is the key to success."

"Do you really think that winning Mrs. Beauchamp's approval is so important to your success? I had always thought winning the admiration of the lady in question was the most important factor," said Tristram.

"And how many ladies have you courted, halfling?"

Tristram glared at him, but Max only chuckled. "No, trust me. I know what I am doing with Mrs. Beauchamp. If I want to wed Miss Philippa Beauchamp, it is through the mother — as unsavory as she may be — that I must go. Marriage is not like in your knightly tales of Sir Milton."

"Perhaps not, but I still think it should be the two parties concerned who are . . . well, involved."

"Never you mind," said Max, giving his cravat a final tug. "There! That is perfect. No, Tristram. All you have to do is tell Miss Beauchamp how much I admire her and how admirable I am. I'll take care of the mother."

"With pleasure," said Tristram.

Half an hour later, Max and Tristram went up the steps to the front door of the Beauchamp town home. The interior was freshly painted and filled with ornate furniture, black lacquered with red and gold dragons painted on the surface. The butler led them straight to the drawing room, where the furnishings were much the same.

Mrs. Beauchamp was seated on a gold silk settee. Her gown was a burnished copper, and planted in her elegant coiffure was a bright orange feather, which waved wildly as she talked.

"Gentlemen, how delightful to see you

both. Let me introduce my little Snookems. Snookems, this handsome man is Mr. Maxwell Darby, and that is his brother Mr. Tristram Darby. Make your bow."

Max and Tristram shared a quick glance before saying politely, "Good afternoon." It was unclear if they were addressing the little black and silver monkey that was bowing repeatedly to them, but the matron chose to think so, and she chortled happily.

"Now, Philippa, you must make your curtsy, and then we will be on our way." She did not pause to see if her daughter obeyed, but the childishly garbed girl bobbed a curtsy which the gentlemen responded to. She said not a word, keeping her head down all the while.

"The carriage was outside when you arrived, was it not, gentlemen?"

"I believe that it was, madam. Allow me to escort you," said Max, hurrying forward to help Mrs. Beauchamp rise and offer his arm. Glancing at his brother, he cocked his head toward Miss Beauchamp, and Tristram offered his arm to the shy miss.

On the doorstep, Max was taken aback when the monkey leaped into his arms.

"Oh, little Snookems wants to go with

us. You will not mind, will you? He is so well behaved."

At this, the well-behaved monkey hopped onto Max's shoulder, and he said tightly, "Of course not, my dear Mrs. Beauchamp." If this was what it took to win the mother's approval, then he would bite his tongue and do it.

"Now, Philippa, you must sit in the rear-facing seat. You know how Snookems gets when he rides backward. And Mr. Tristram, you sit beside her — that's a good boy."

Tristram grumbled under his breath, but he took the rear-facing seat, leaving Max to sit beside the pushy matron.

"Isn't this delightful," declared Mrs. Beauchamp as they got under way. "Tell me, Mr. Darby, how do you feel about the theater?"

"I enjoy it very much," Max replied while sending a silent signal to his brother that he should pay attention to the younger Beauchamp lady.

"It is splendid weather we are having, is it not?" asked Tristram.

"Yes, sir," she replied, never lifting her face.

"I understand that it is quite unusual for this time of year to have had as many sunny days as we have."

"I . . . I believe so."

"Your dear brother has offered to escort me to the theater tomorrow night, Mr. Darby," said Mrs. Beauchamp.

"And your charming daughter, too, of course," said Max hurriedly.

"What? Oh, certainly. You will agree to come, too, will you not, Mr. Darby? It would be rather awkward without you. I mean, rather like having uneven numbers at a dinner party."

"Yes, certainly I will come," he replied, glancing at the girl.

"Then it is all settled. Now, do tell me, Mr. Darby," she said, taking Max's arm and leaning against him, "is that not the most atrocious bonnet you have ever seen? Whatever could Lady Murray have been thinking?"

"Lady Murray?" asked Max.

"Yes, there in the landaulet. You remember her. We attended her ball the other night. It is too late. Perhaps when we pass them on the way out of the park."

"My brother is quite a good rider, Miss Beauchamp," said Tristram.

"Is he?"

"Yes, he's rather a Corinthian, you know. Riding, shooting, all sorts of sports, but especially the horses."

"Horses frighten me," said the girl, daring a glance up at him.

"Snookems, sit still, do! Please help me hold onto him, Mr. Darby. Dare I call you Max? It is so confusing having two Mr. Darbys in the carriage."

"Certainly, madam," said Max, grinning at Tristram as he corralled the little beast, holding it rather forcefully in his lap.

"What do you like to do, Mr. Darby? I know you are an artist, but what else do you enjoy?" asked the girl, again glancing up at him with those huge blue eyes.

"Oh, I am a bit of a dull stick. Nothing so exciting as Max. I hate riding, and shooting gives me the headache, not to mention having to pick up dead rabbits and such."

"Oh, dear," she said, her hand to her throat.

"I . . . actually, I write. I also paint, but I have not been trained, so I am afraid my efforts are quite amateurish."

"You write, too? Oh, how lovely. What do you write?"

"Poetry and . . . and novels. I have written a novel that is . . . that is, I should not be saying this to you since it is considered gauche for a gentleman to sell his skills, but I am rather proud of it," said Tristram, looking down at the little puzzled frown creasing her brow. "I have a novel that has been printed and is even now in the booksellers."

"Oh, how extraordinary."

"What is the play tomorrow night, Philippa? I know that I mentioned it to you, but I cannot think now . . ."

The girl spared a glance for her mother and said, "*Othello,* Mama. What is the name of your novel, Mr. Darby? I must purchase it."

"Nonsense, you needn't do that."

"Oh, but I want to!" she breathed.

"Really? Well, then, you shan't buy it. I have a copy at home. I will send it around to you, or bring it myself."

"Bring it yourself," she whispered. "We are *not* going out this evening."

"Yes, but . . ."

"I usually stroll in the garden before dinner, around seven o'clock."

Tristram glanced down into those blue orbs and nodded. Glancing up, he found his brother's blue eyes fixed on him, and he smiled nervously. Looking away, he turned his attention to the passing scenery.

Lady Murray was Mrs. O'Connor's older

sister. She had centered her life on London Society. Though she had opposed her little sister's marriage to the penniless Kieran O'Connor, she had not cut the ties. She had visited Ireland several times through the years and had encouraged her sister to visit her in London. Lady Murray's invitations had fallen on deaf ears until Mrs. O'Connor had decided her daughter needed to be settled.

Neither lady guessed that the object of their designs had decided against wedding, at least in England. Kate was not against the concept, and perhaps she would discover some heretofore unknown gentleman to win her heart when she returned to Ireland. Whatever happened, though, she was determined to go back home to Ireland.

On the surface, Kate was quite amenable, wearing one of her new carriage dresses and donning a fetching bonnet. She granted each gentleman a mechanical smile, but there was none of the animation in her expression that drew people to her. Her aunt and mother, however, were well satisfied that she was behaving exactly as she ought.

The carriage ride might have ended without incident, but for a nearby commotion. The snaking line of carriages came to a halt in both directions.

"What in heaven's name could be the matter?" declared Lady Murray, rising from her seat. Her lips were pursed in disapproval, and her bonnet, which boasted a banana and cluster of dangling grapes, loomed in the air for everyone to see.

"Appears t' be some sort of animal, m'lady," said her coachman, craning his head to see around a high-perch phaeton.

"Well, go around them," she commanded.

The coachman pulled out from behind the phaeton, giving the ladies a better view, and Lady Murray screeched, "Halt!"

The animal in question appeared at the door of the open landaulet and let out a piercing screech.

"Here now!" yelled the coachman, turning in his seat and diving for the black and silver monkey. He landed squarely on the laps of Kate's mother and aunt, his legs thrashing in the air.

With a flash of petticoats and ankles, Kate jumped off the carriage seat and into the driver's seat, steadying the horses.

"Get him!" screamed another feminine voice.

Kate whirled around. Mrs. Beauchamp was climbing into their carriage, wielding her parasol to pummel the beleaguered coachman, while tearing at Lady Murray's bonnet, where the offending monkey had taken up residence and was holding on for dear life.

"Get off!" yelled Kate's mother, using her own parasol to parry the wild woman's thrusts.

"Give . . . me . . . my . . . Snookems!" screamed Mrs. Beauchamp.

Gaping at the scene, but unable to leave the team, Kate watched the monkey leap into the air and dive onto the seat beside her, all the while clutching the mangled silk grapes from her aunt's bonnet.

"Come here," she said firmly, stifling a laugh when the little beast jumped onto her shoulder.

Oblivious of her pet's escape, Mrs. Beauchamp continued her assault, screeching like a banshee. Kate was dimly aware of other spectators — some laughing, some screaming — but her concern was all for her mother.

Then she saw him, like a knight of old, running toward her, sweeping Mrs. Beauchamp into his arms, and backing away. Almost throwing the outraged matron into her carriage, he returned and held up his hands for the mischievous monkey. Kate handed the animal to him as his laughing blue eyes met hers. Smiling, she answered his wink with one of her own. Then he was gone.

The poor coachman, scarlet with embarrassment, managed to right himself and climb back on his seat, relieving Kate of the reins. She hopped to the ground and entered the landaulet more decorously than she had vacated it. Then she set about soothing her mother's lacerated sensibilities while fishing in her aunt's reticule for Lady Murray's smelling salts.

While her mother was occupied in reviving her dear sister, Kate straightened, her gaze immediately drawn to that one figure amongst the crowd. She watched in admiration as Max Darby soothed the monkey and Mrs. Beauchamp while his brother, Tristram, tried to stem the flood of tears from Miss Philippa Beauchamp. She did not envy either gentleman his task. As their carriage passed by, Kate gave him a little wave, which Max answered with a nod.

She rather thought Max Darby was more like Sir Milton than his brother Tristram was. Max was certainly more of a take-charge sort of person. In contrast, his brother looked almost as shaken as the two ladies.

"I think we should go straight home," she said to the coachman.

"Yes, miss," he replied, pulling his hat down firmly on his head. "Right away."

Max hurried into the garden when he returned home. He knew Kate would come, drawn by the same irresistible force to share the afternoon's hilarity with him. It was almost dark, but he felt sure she would be waiting. She was the sort of girl who would not be put off by a bit of gloom. Recalling the way those green eyes had sparkled when he had taken the monkey from her, he could not associate gloom with her in any setting.

"Kate?" he said, forgetting both propriety and their roles as Sir Milton and Iseult. This was no time for charades.

"Sir Milton?" came the reply, her voice already filled with laughter.

"What? No . . . dash it! This is intolerable. I want to see you. I'm going to come around to the front door."

"Not now. It is not the proper time, and Mama has had enough excitement for one day. She is still a little delicate."

"Well, this is deuced inconvenient, Kate."

"I know. I . . . sh! Wait. Someone is

coming. Hello, Mr. Taggert."

Max strained to hear her voice as she turned away.

"Afternoon, miss. Was you lookin' for somewat?"

"No, I was just out for a stroll."

"Oh. I thought ye might be lookin' for the gate. It's farther down, ye know."

"Gate?"

"Yes, between this house an' the next. It used t' stay open on account o' th' two families were related. It's shut now, but if you want . . ."

"Oh, yes, please, Mr. Taggert. Could you unlock it for me?"

"I'd be happy to, miss. It's right 'ere."

"Thank you, Mr. Taggert."

"Yer welcome, miss. I'll see that it stays unlocked."

The gate creaked as it swung open, and then Kate stepped through the opening. Max extended his hands and she took them, letting him draw her close. Her eyes grew wide.

In the fading light, he smiled down at her and said, "I do hope you are not disappointed that I am not Tristram."

"Not at all, though I must admit that I am a bit surprised," she said, returning his smile.

He tucked her hand into the crook of his arm and led her along the wall. "Come over here. Here's the bench where I sit."

When they were side by side, he kept her hand in his. Turning slightly so that he faced her, Max said, "I have to confess that I was not the one you spoke to that first night, the one who first called you Iseult."

"I thought you were different after that night. It wasn't just your voice. Your brother is more poetic. What happened to him? Did I frighten him?"

"No, he is just forgetful. When Tris is reading or writing something, he forgets everything, including the prettiest horse-woman I have ever seen."

Without a hint of coyness, she ignored his compliment and said, "So he *is* Mr. Poorman, the author of the Sir Milton novel I am reading."

"You're reading it?" said Max. "I hadn't thought about people actually reading the thing."

Kate chuckled and said, "You needn't sound so surprised, Mr. Darby. Some people do read novels."

"Certainly, but to think that you would have chosen to read that particular one at this particular time. It is quite as-tounding."

"Not really. When I spoke to the clerk at Hatchard's — who was reading it also, by the way — he mentioned that the hero was Sir Milton. That caught my interest immediately. When I discovered that the heroine was Iseult, I put two and two together."

"So what do you think of my little brother's writing?"

"It is most entertaining. I feel as if I am on the crusade alongside Sir Milton. Your brother is quite talented."

"Yes, he is the talented brother. My twin is the sensible one."

"And you?"

"Me? I am the hotheaded, impulsive, daredevil brother."

"Rather like Sir Milton," she said, smiling up at him.

"I couldn't say. I'm afraid I haven't read Tristram's stories."

"You should do so. After seeing you in action this afternoon, I rather think you must be the inspiration for Sir Milton. I suppose when you took over his role at the garden wall, perhaps it was not such a great deception."

"Perhaps," said Max, inching closer to her.

Suddenly she shivered, and he noticed for the first time that she was not wearing a cloak. Making a move to shed his own coat, she stilled him by rising.

"I should be going. My father would not approve of this."

"Why? Surely there is nothing wrong with neighbors . . ."

"Paying a call through the front door," she said with a chuckle.

Max rose and bowed over her hand. "Then we will treat this as a formal call, Miss O'Connor."

Kate gave a gurgle of laughter and a small curtsy before turning away. At the garden gate, she looked back at him through the gloom.

"Tomorrow at noon we will be expecting you, Sir Milton."

"I will not fail, fair Iseult," he replied, still smiling, even after she had gone.

Max sat down on the stone bench again, leaning his head against the garden wall. He felt sure of himself with Miss O'Connor. She was not some missish chit of a girl. She was fully grown and knew what a man wanted of a woman. He felt confident that, given his expertise and her willingness, they could enjoy a cozy relationship while each one of them pursued his objectives. At the end of the Little Season, he would have secured a wealthy bride in Miss Beauchamp and Kate . . . Kate would be going home to Ireland or to the home of some insipid fellow with more money than horse sense.

Why did he suddenly feel like punching a hole in the stone wall?

Four

Miss Philippa Beauchamp glanced left and then right. No one was coming from the front of the house. The kitchen servants were busy preparing dinner. So far, so good. Taking a deep breath, she gathered her skirts in her hand and scurried out the back door, praying no one would look out the windows and discover her flight.

Her breath coming in tiny rasps, she paused to get her bearings. She had seen the gate that led to the lane behind the house, though she had never ventured to open it. What if it were locked? The impossible thought made her tremble, but she forged ahead, determined to attain her goal.

"Miss Beauchamp?"

The voice made her gasp, but she stumbled through the gloom toward the sound. Then strong hands held her steady, and she exhaled a deep sigh of relief.

"Mr. Darby, I am glad you found your way," she breathed.

His profile was in silhouette against the darkening skies.

"So am I," he said, smiling down at her. "I . . . I have your book."

"Good. Perhaps you would care to sit down?" Philippa grimaced. She was acting a complete ninnyhammer, and she was not usually one. Well, she corrected, not usually a *complete* one.

"I would love to. I think I saw a bench over here."

They came upon the small arbor, and Philippa said, "There is only the one seat, I'm afraid."

"Then you must take it," said Tristram gallantly.

"No, for you are so tall, I would not be able to see your face. You sit down, and . . . I . . . I shall . . ."

"Perch on my knee," he said, his voice full of honesty and kindness, and she knew he could not be wanting the same things from her those other men, her mother's *friends,* had wanted.

Blushing, Philippa did as he said. She was steadied on her perch by a gentle pressure from his hand on her waist. With the other, he placed the book in her lap.

"I do hope you will like it."

"I know I shall since you wrote it," she replied, turning to face him.

In the somber shadows, their faces were

so close, she could feel his gentle breaths. Leaning toward him was the most natural thing. Their lips touched. His hand moved up her back and cradled her against him as she leaned her head against his broad chest.

"I hope you will not think me too forward," she said finally, lifting her head to gaze into his eyes. The moon was rising, and she could see indecision written there.

With a little grimace, he shifted so that she was forced to rise. Standing in front of her, his hands clutched hers as she held the book.

"Miss Beauchamp . . . Philippa, I . . . cannot betray my . . . I cannot."

He took a step away from her and dropped his hands to his sides. He might as well have crossed a desert, for when next he spoke, his voice was dry and empty of all emotion.

"The hero of the book is Sir Milton. He is a capital sort of fellow, modeled after my brother Max, who is also a capital sort of fellow. He is not the sort who would trifle with someone else's . . . I must go. I do hope you will think of Max while you are reading this. He is the very best person I know, full of all sorts of noble ideals and qualities. He would never dream of betraying a trust. Never."

"Mr. Darby . . . Tristram?"

"I must go. I . . . I should never have come."

And then he was gone. Philippa sat down on the little chair and cried — small, tiny sobs that befitted a girl who was small and tiny. Inside, however, she was quite certain her heart was breaking, and she wished she *were* a complete ninnyhammer, because then she would not have understood what Tristram was saying.

It was his brother who was courting her, not sweet, gentle Tristram. Tristram might be attracted to her, but he was not interested in taking her as his wife.

At this realization, Philippa thought her heart really would break!

That night, at the invitation of the Marquess of Cravenwell, Max and Tristram set out for dinner at White's, one of the most fashionable men's clubs in London. Gambling was the main activity, especially in the evening, but neither Darby brother was inclined to join in the play.

As they entered the hallowed portals, Max said, "What the devil has you so peevish? You have been frowning ever since you came home this afternoon."

"Why shouldn't I be cross? What is the meaning of this summons? I mean, does the dirty marquess want to inspect us? I should think he knows what we look like by now."

"Perhaps he invited us to be polite," said Max, grinning unabashedly.

Tristram could not help but smile at his brother's nonsensical comment. Then he spied the marquess and his father.

"Devil take me! The old fool's playing cards with the marquess again!" exclaimed Tristram. "We will never see the light of day!"

"I wonder if there is a way for us to disown him?" quipped Max. "There, that's better. Might as well grin and bear it. Come on, Tris."

The viscount sat opposite the marquess, his nose in a hand of cards, a glass of brandy at his elbow, and a smile on his face.

"Sit down, lads," he said, motioning them forward.

"And be quiet," growled the marquess.

"Do not be offended by your host's incivility. He is not accustomed to losing, especially to me," said Viscount Tavistoke with a chuckle.

"Wouldn't be tonight except that he is

having the most damnable run of luck," snapped the marquess.

"Piquet always was your game, Papa," said Max, taking a chair on his father's right side while Tristram still stood, gazing around the club.

"Sit down, young chub. Hasn't anyone ever told you it ain't polite to stand over people when they're playing cards? Thought a son of Tavistoke here would know better."

"And so he does," said the viscount as Tristram slipped into the fourth chair at the table.

"Sorry. I wasn't looking at your cards, either of you. I just hadn't been here before, and . . ."

"Well, you mustn't even think of drawing this place," said the rude marquess, jabbing Tristram in the chest with one bony finger. "It would play havoc with the members!"

"I don't see why. It's nothing that isn't going on in a dozen other clubs at this very moment," said Tristram, glaring at the older man.

"Oh, so this one's decided to take the bit in his mouth and run with it, has he?" said the marquess. "It would be well for you to remember, my boy, who is footing the bil for this second foray into the Marriage Mart — a second foray that would not have been necessary if you had taken care of business the first time instead of drawing all your little pictures. That didn't get you very far, now, did it?"

Tristram's chest swelled with indignation, but Max beat him to it by saying casually, "True, and it has made me wonder why, my lord, you didn't simply have our father put in debtor's prison after last Season. That was originally your plan, was it not?"

It was the marquess's turn to glare, but he said nothing.

Max smiled and continued, "Why do we not quit our squabbling? Your note said you wished to know about our progress, and I am prepared to enlighten you."

"Exactly," said the viscount, playing his final card with a flourish. "I think we are finished playing piquet for the moment. It is too pleasant an evening to argue."

"What has you in such a good mood, Papa?" asked Max.

It was the marquess who responded instead with a cackle, and said, "He's happy because he has taken my money and because Lady Anne cannot possibly appear o tell him to stop playing cards, blowing a

112

cloud, or drinking his fill."

"Demmed interfering female," muttered the viscount. "But let's not talk about her. Dinner, I think, and a bottle of their finest?"

With another of his dry cackles, the marquess nodded, crooking his finger at a waiter and growling out his orders for their dinner.

"Your sons are trying my patience, Tavistoke," he said over the first course of mulligatawny soup, a poached salmon, and roasted pears.

"Have they not been trying mine for some thirty years?"

"Only nine and twenty, Papa," said Max. Looking his father in the eye, he added, "I am certain the tables have been turned any number of times."

The marquess chortled happily over this, saying, "This one is a bit too cocky, but the other one . . ."

"The other one has a name, my lord. You may use it or not, but I refuse to be spoken about as if I were not even here," said Tristram, rising out of his seat.

"Ah, so he does have a backbone. Good! I was afraid he was nothing but books and drawing. Sit down, do."

Tristram receded onto the soft leather

chair, though he remained tight-lipped. The marquess, however, had returned his attention to Max.

"So tell us, my boy, have you found a likely candidate?"

Lowering his voice so that it did not carry to the other tables, Max said, "Miss Philippa Beauchamp."

"Not Beastly Beauchamp," groaned his father.

"Beastly? What the devil are you talking about, Papa? Miss Beauchamp is an angel, a perfect angel!"

"But the mother, boy. Egads! How can we ever stomach such a creature in our family?"

"I am not marrying the mother," snapped Max.

The marquess started to laugh and clapped Max on the back. "Good for you, my boy! The mother is a vulgar mushroom, but if you can land the girl, her father's like to pay a pretty penny. Well done!" Snapping his bony fingers, he signaled the servant, saying, "Champagne! We must celebrate!"

With their champagne, they set upon the second remove of braised lamb cutlets, duck à l'orange, a plum tart, and various side dishes. The marquess — and therefore the viscount — were in such charity with Max that they refrained from asking the same question of Tristram, who sat quietly, his eyes never leaving the plate that was put in front of him.

"So tell me, my boy, when can we expect to see an announcement in the papers?" asked the viscount, rubbing his hands together as if already counting the marriage settlements.

"I should think within a couple of weeks. Mustn't appear too eager, you know," said Max. "We are to join them at the theater tomorrow night."

"Capital!" said the marquess. "You and I will attend, too, Tavistoke. My box is opposite theirs, so there's no reason we cannot enjoy the show."

"We will be there to cheer you on, my boy." As if suddenly recalling that he had two sons sitting at the table, the viscount slew around and fixed Tristram with a martial stare. "What about you, Tris? What have you to say for yourself?"

The words were slurred. His father was well past it. All he had to do was fob him off with some tale, but that was not Tristram's way. Honesty was forever his downfall.

"Me, sir? I have nothing to report. I

cannot tell you when or where I shall have something to report. I find this entire discussion reprehensible."

"Here now," said his father.

"No, let the boy speak," said the marquess, skewering Tristram with his beady eyes. "Tell us, my boy, what is so reprehensible about what your brother is doing? What any other gentleman or lady is doing here in London for the Little Season? Are you so far above all the rest of them?"

Tristram turned scarlet and rose. "Not above them, my lord, but I will not be trotted out like a horse at Tattersall's. I will take my time and make my choice because it is what I want, not simply to please the likes of . . . Society."

He turned on his heel and stalked away, but not before hearing Max say quietly, "I should follow him. Good evening, gentlemen. Thank you for your hospitality, my lord."

"See what you can do to straighten up that young cawker," the marquess snapped, his voice rising so that Tristram could hear him. "Otherwise, I'll not be responsible for the consequences."

Max soon caught up with Tristram as he trotted down the front steps.

He ignored Max's calls until, finally, he

whirled and said through gritted teeth, "Just leave me alone, Max. You go on back to those two . . ."

"Whatever is the matter with you, Tris? You are usually more coolheaded than this. Don't let Cravenwell rattle you. He's nothing but a greedy old good-for-nothing, you know that. And we both know what Papa is, and what is behind his wanting us to both marry well. You should not let them ruin our fun."

Tristram looked his older brother in the eye and then shook his head. It was on the tip of his tongue to tell his brother that he could not have Philippa Beauchamp, that Tristram wanted the beauty for himself. On the tip of his tongue, but it could go no farther. Max had laid his claim first.

"You do not understand, Max, and I cannot explain it to you. Not now. Just leave me to work things out for myself, won't you? Until then, I will be better off on my own."

To salve his brother's concern, Tristram offered his hand. After a moment, Max took it, gave it a firm shake, and held it.

"You're sure?"

Tris nodded, and Max released him, pausing another moment before turning back to White's with its leather cushions and clouds of smoke. Tristram watched him go, answering Max's final wave with a little nod before his brother entered the building and was gone from view.

Turning, Tristram began the short walk home. How could he have let things go so far? Not that anything had happened — except that brief kiss. Tristram closed his eyes, remembering the sweet taste of her lips on his.

Who would have thought that he would fall head over heels for a chit barely out of the schoolroom? One who was so shy she could barely muster two sentences in a row. One who was so securely under the thumb of that frightful mother!

Philippa needed rescuing, and Max was the one to do the job. He was, after all, the brother who never shrank from daring deeds. How could he ever hope to compare with Max in that area? Not to mention that he would never stand in Max's way. Max had claimed her first, and honor forbade him from interfering.

No, Max was the right one to rescue Philippa. When the time came, he would face down the dragon-mother like a knight of old. Sweet, innocent Philippa would be much better off with a hero like Max.

Tristram entered the house and went

straight to the sideboard to pour himself a large brandy.

"Oh, I *am* sorry, sir. I did not hear you come in. Would you like something to eat, something to go along with that?" asked Barton, looking from the full glass to his youngest charge.

"No, this is all I need. You can go to bed, Barton," said Tristram.

"Thank you, sir, but I would be remiss in my duties if I did so at such an early hour. I will be available if either you or Master Max needs me."

Tristram ignored the servant and sprawled on the sofa, putting his feet on the table before it.

"Shall I just help you with those boots, Master Tristram?" said Barton, hurrying forward and lifting one leg to remove the offending footgear. When he was finished with that, he said, "I shall bring your dressing gown, sir. You will be much more comfortable in that."

"Suit yourself," came the bald reply as Tristram finished off the contents of his glass.

When Barton returned a few seconds later, Tristram had risen and returned to the sideboard to replenish his glass. He paused in pouring to allow Barton to help him out of his coat and into the silk dressing gown. When Barton turned him toward the sofa with a gentle shove, Tristram did not balk in the least. The brandy was already warming him from the inside, dulling the pain in his heart. When Barton handed him another glass, filled only halfway to the top, he accepted it with a smile.

"Thank you, Barton."

"My pleasure, sir. Call if you need anything else, Master Tristram."

When he was alone again, Tristram took another pull on the heady liquid and muttered, "Would call in a second if I weren't past help. Dashed honor. It hasn't been good for much of anything up to now, and now it's just standing in my way."

Another deep drink, and he moaned, "Oh, Philippa, my sweet, dear Philippa."

"Get up, slugabed!"

This pronouncement was accompanied by a flood of light as Max threw back the window curtains.

"Arghhh," groaned the figure in the bed, pulling his pillow over his head.

"Come along, Tris. We have people to see. I have an appointment with our charming Iseult next door. You should come and meet her, too."

The mumble that came out from under the pillow was indecipherable, and Max pulled the pillow away, tossing it on the floor.

"You are the one who started all that Iseult nonsense. The least you can do is come with me to pay a proper call. I think you will be delighted by Miss O'Connor."

"I very much doubt it," grumbled Tristram, glaring at his brother and holding his head. "Go on alone. I'll meet her later."

"No, you will not. I expect you to be up and dressed in the next twenty minutes."

"Papa! I cannot believe you would do such a despicable thing! And you were not even going to tell me!"

"Kate, do not raise your voice to your father," said Mrs. O'Connor, reaching out to restrain her daughter.

Kate leaped to her feet, out of her mother's reach, and faced her father squarely.

"I cannot believe you were going to sell Early Girl and not even tell me! Why not sell one of the others?"

"I know you are upset, Mary Kate, but it cannot be helped. You have no idea what this Season is costing us. I have to sell your mare if we are to continue here. If there were some sign that you had encouraged some suitable young man and I could see the end in sight, perhaps I would not be forced to do so," said the man, running a hand through his sparse red hair.

Her breasts heaving, Kate pursed her lips. She had no answer for her father. She had not encouraged any of the young men she had met because she did not wish to marry them, did not wish to find an English husband and live in England, but she could hardly tell her father this. He would be furious.

As her tears began to flow, her father said sorrowfully, "There now, my pet, do not cry so. You'll see. 'Twill all be worth it when you meet that special young man."

"Oh, Papa," wailed Kate, hurrying from the room. "You . . . you don't understand anything!"

She ran up the stairs to her bedroom and shut the door. Sitting on the side of the bed, she kicked at the carpet and dried her tears. She had long since learned that it did no good to go against her father when he made plans to buy or sell a horse. It was business to him, and that meant it did not concern her.

But this was Early Girl, her own mare. Since they had won Thunderlight, she had dreamed about the beautiful colts he and her sweet mare would have. The thought of losing her was intolerable!

Rising, Kate straightened the habit she still wore and went quietly down the stairs to the front hall. Her father had forbidden her visiting the stables since they arrived in London, but she had to see Early Girl one more time.

Kate could hear her parents still conversing in the drawing room. Silently, she opened the door and slipped outside only to find herself chest to chest with her neighbor.

He took a step back and swept off his hat, saying, "Good morning, Miss O'Connor. I have come to pay you that call."

Kate burst into loud, wet tears.

Completely disconcerted, Max turned to Tristram, who was only then joining him on the steps.

"My dear girl, let us go back inside," said Tristram, taking her by the elbow.

She wrenched away from him, putting one gloved hand on Max's chest and whispering, "I . . . I cannot go back inside now."

"Then she'll have to come with us," said Max, taking her arm and leading her down the steps, along the pavement, and, after a quick glance around the small square, up their steps and safely inside.

"Dear me!" exclaimed Barton.

"Just find some, uh, whatever it is you give a lady in these circumstances and pour her a glass, Barton," said Max, leading Kate to the sofa and sitting down by her side.

Her sobs had been replaced by little sniffles, and he offered his handkerchief to her, giving her shoulder a bracing pat.

"There, there," he said.

"Oh, Mr. Darby, I . . . I am so sorry," she said, giving him a watery smile. "I thought I had myself quite in hand."

"Nonsense. You have nothing to apologize to me about. We are happy to help in any way we can," said Max.

"No, you do not understand."

"Perhaps you could enlighten us, Miss O'Connor," said Tristram.

Her glance showed that Kate had forgotten all about his presence. Barton arrived with the promised beverage, handed it to Max, and then backed away.

Max sniffed the amber liquid and gave a grunt. Handing her the sherry, he said,

"Drink this right down. It may not solve any problems, but I find a good drink can clear the head like nothing else."

She took a sip, wrinkling her nose. He touched her hand, and she took another swallow before returning it to him.

"Now, what can your two Sir Miltons do to come to your aid, fair Iseult?" asked Max, the question making her smile.

"I do not think there is anything you can do, Mr. Darby. It is about my mare, Early Girl. Papa is going to sell her."

"All this over a horse," muttered Tristram, earning a glare from both occupants of the couch. He sank onto a chair and pursed his lips.

"The mare you brought from home? Why ever would he do such a thing?" asked Max.

"It is money again. It is always money."

"Well, yes, it does often come down to that," said Max glumly. "Still, there must be some other way. Why does he not sell Thunderlight? You have no great emotional attachment to him yet, do you?"

"No, not really. Oh, he is a sweet goer, but it is not the same as when one has watched a horse be foaled. You spend hours earning her trust, gentling her, teaching her . . . I am sorry. I am just rattling on," said Kate.

"Not at all. I know just how you feel. So what about Thunderlight?"

"I asked Papa, but he reminded me that our stallion is getting on up there, and that we need new blood in the line, and Thunderlight . . . well, you can imagine how delighted my father was to win him."

Max nodded and said, "Just so. Then we must think of something else. When is he going to put the mare on the block?"

"Thursday, at Tattersall's, and being a lady, I cannot even go and watch," said Kate.

"Would you wish to do so?" asked Max.

"Oh, yes. At least I would know what sort of person has bought her. Oh, Mr. Darby, I do not know if I can bear it," said Kate, taking his hand and squeezing it.

The tears threatened to overflow, and it seemed only natural when he pulled her against his chest to comfort her. His arms around her, Kate felt the weight of the world slip from her shoulders. Mr. Darby, Mr. *Max* Darby, would think of something.

A moment passed, and she straightened and whispered, "I should be going."

"What? Oh, yes, but perhaps it would be best if you go back through the garden gate," said Max, rising and giving her his hand.

"What garden gate?" asked Tristram.

Ignoring him, Kate agreed and allowed Max to lead her into the garden. At the gate, he bowed over her hand, kissing the back of it lightly.

"Never fear, fair Iseult, Sir Milton will see you clear of this bramble."

"Thank you, Sir Milton," she said, managing a smile for him before slipping through the garden gate.

When Max returned to the drawing room a few minutes later, his brow was furrowed as he pondered Kate's problem.

After several moments, he snapped his fingers and said, "I have it, Tris. I will arrange another match race for Thunderlight. With the winnings, Kate's father will have another horse, a different horse, to sell at Tattersall's on Thursday!"

Tristram groaned, "Max, this is where you got into trouble last time. What's more, it is how Miss O'Connor's father won the stallion in the first place."

"Yes, but I was not riding him. Do not concern yourself over this, Tristram. I will handle everything. You'll see! Everything will be fine!"

"Have you lost your mind?" asked Tristram.

"Not at all," Max replied, sitting down at the desk which was usually Tristram's spot. He picked up a leaf of paper and then the pen, thinking for a moment before dipping it in the inkstand and beginning to write.

Tristram wandered closer to peered over his shoulder.

"Palmer? Nance? What the devil are you doing?"

"I am making a list of people who make a habit of purchasing horses that are too much for them to handle. They like their cattle to be the best, the fastest, but on the whole, they are the most abysmal horsemen. They do not realize this, of course, so it makes them easier, uh, targets."

"I didn't think Palmer was like that," said Tristram.

"Perhaps not as much as some of the others, but he irritated me the other night at Lady Murray's ball when he mentioned *my* losing Thunderlight — as if *I* ever would have lost him!"

"Max, use your common sense for a moment. This is wrong."

"Wrong? To help a damsel in distress? I thought that is what you are always going on about in those stories of yours. And if you base this Sir Milton on me, then you must know that I will do whatever it takes to help the damsel."

"But Max, Thunderlight is not yours to lose, as some of these gentlemen may point out to you."

"No, but with Kate there as the owner, they'll bite. At least one of them will. Don't worry, little brother. I know what I am doing."

"Seems to me that is the same thing Papa would say just before he loses another wager," said Tristram, not even flinching when Max pushed back the chair abruptly and glared at him. "I am just telling you what I see."

His teeth clenched, Max ground out, "Do not ever compare me to our father like that again. I am not some fool throwing away good money after bad. I would never consider this if it weren't for Kate. I get nothing out of this."

"Nothing? What about Miss O'Connor's admiration? Have you stopped to ask yourself what she thinks about your role in this? Do you wonder if perhaps she will view this as tantamount to a proposal of marriage?"

"A proposal . . . bah! You are well out on that score!"

"Am I? Will she not ask herself why her handsome neighbor is going to such extraordinary lengths to help her keep her beloved mare? Might she not think it is because you are trying to win her affection?"

"You know, this habit you have adopted of asking questions one after the other is very annoying." Looking away, Max took out his handkerchief and mopped his brow. "Do you really think I am encouraging her to think that?"

"I do," said Tristram.

"Then I will have to talk to her, to explain to her that . . . that it has nothing to do with . . . that if she has any idea of marriage to me, then . . ."

Max spun on his heel and marched to the door.

"Where are you going now?" asked Tristram.

"Next door. I never did pay that call. I think it is time."

"Do you want me to come with you?"

"No, I think one Darby brother paying an unannounced call on our neighbor is quite enough." Pausing at the door, Max grinned and added, "Besides which, I really do not need any witnesses to my foolishness."

Max hurried out the door and down the

front steps, retracing his path. This time, his knock was answered by a respectable-looking footman who took his card and asked him to wait in the hall while he ascertained if his mistress was receiving.

A moment later, the servant returned and ushered Max up the stairs to the drawing room.

"Good afternoon, Mr. Darby. I have heard a great deal about you," said a tall, thin man with wispy red hair and a mild Irish accent.

"Good afternoon, Mr. O'Connor. I have heard a thing or two about you, too," he replied.

"Allow me to introduce my good wife."

Max executed a bow over her hand and said, "How do you do, Mrs. O'Connor. After our little contretemps in the park yesterday, I feel I already know you."

Her laugh was musical, and she motioned to him to take the chair beside the sofa. "I was never so pleased to see a stranger, I can tell you, Mr. Darby. You saved all of us from that horrible woman. Oh, I do beg your pardon. She must be a friend of yours."

"A . . . an acquaintance, merely. I . . . I have a particular interest in her daughter," he confessed baldly. There, that should quickly get back to Kate, and she would know he did not have any designs on her in that respect.

"Oh? Should we offer you congratulations?"

"No, no, not yet. I have only . . . but there, this is hardly a proper topic for us, having only just met."

"Quite right," said Mr. O'Connor. "The young man has probably called to see if he can visit the stables and see his old horse, Thunderlight."

"That would be wonderful, but I am also calling on your daughter. I met her at Lady Murray's ball," he lied. "And then yesterday, in the park, I was quite impressed with her quick thinking, which kept the carriage horses from bolting. I hope she did not suffer any lasting discomfort."

"From holding the ribbons for a couple of silly carriage horses? Hardly likely, my boy. Obviously, you are not well acquainted with my Kate," said the father with pride.

"As I said, sir, I have met her only twice," said Max, looking around the drawing room as if expecting to discover her lurking in a far corner. "Is she here this afternoon?"

"Why don't you ring for the footman to

go up and see, my dear?" said Mrs. O'Connor. While her husband did as she requested, she asked, "Are you visiting in London, Mr. Darby, or do you make your home here?"

"Actually, my brother and I are visiting, and as luck would have it, we are next door to you."

"How extraordinary. Then you must come for tea one afternoon, both you and your brother."

"That would be wonderful, ma'am. I shall look forward to it."

"So you are also a great lover of horses," she commented.

"Yes, they are a passion of mine. I'm afraid while I am in London, I make do with horses from the Marquess of Cravenwell's stable. He is . . . an old family friend."

"I see," said the matron.

As usual, mention of the marquess in polite company put an end to most conversation. The man's reputation was legendary.

"Kate will be right down. She said she wants to thank you for rescuing them from the beast," said Mr. O'Connor.

The glimmer of a smile crossed Max's face at this. O'Connor had not specified whether the beast he mentioned was the pet monkey or Mrs. Beauchamp. Max rather thought he would say the latter.

"You're a trifle large to be racing, but you must have a way with the horses if the stories I have heard about all those match races you won last spring are true, Mr. Darby."

"I do not know what you have heard, Mr. O'Connor, but I did manage to win every time. I think it was due more to Thunderlight than to me."

"Spoken like a true horseman," said the older man with a nod of approval. "I have to admit that I am quite happy you were not riding the stallion the day I set my gelding against him. It might have turned out quite differently."

"No doubt about it," said Max cheerfully.

"You're sure about that?" said the Irishman.

"Well, there is only one way to tell, isn't there? I could ride Thunderlight against your gelding and see what happened."

O'Connor slapped his thigh and said, "By Jove, so you could! We may well have to arrange that, my boy."

"Ah, here is our Kate," said Mrs. O'Connor.

Max rose until Kate had taken the seat

beside her mother.

"Kate, I understand you met Mr. Darby at your aunt's ball. You did not mention it that evening."

"I met so many people," she said, smiling at him.

Max returned that smile. "We did not quite understand that we lived next door to each other, or I would have called before. I trust you suffered no lasting harm yesterday . . . in the park," he added when she looked puzzled.

"Oh, no, I am fine, thank you. How kind of you to call and inquire, Mr. Darby."

"It has been a pleasure becoming acquainted with your charming mother and father."

"This is the young man who used to ride our Thunderlight," said her father.

"Indeed? You must miss him terribly," said Kate, her green eyes dancing.

"As anyone would, who truly cared for a horse," replied Max. "Do you ride, Miss O'Connor?"

Her father snorted, and Kate said politely, "Yes, I do, Mr. Darby."

"Perhaps we might go for a ride in the park one afternoon."

"That would be delightful, Mr. Darby."

"On Thursday, perhaps?"

"That would be all right, would it not, Mama?"

"Well, I suppose so, dear," said the matron, fixing Max with a puzzled frown. "Though we shall understand, of course, if Mr. Darby has other interests that prevent him from escorting you."

"Other interests? Why, I cannot think of anything. Do you prefer to ride in the morning or the afternoon?"

"Shall we say eleven o'clock?" she said.

"Eleven it is," replied Max, rising to leave.

Bowing to the ladies, he mouthed the word "garden" and made his departure.

Kate nodded and bade him good-bye.

"I am sorry it took me so long," whispered Kate, joining Max on the bench on his side of the garden wall. Seeing his open, handsome face made her heart dance, and she pursed her lips and frowned, trying to quell this madness. She hardly knew the man!

"It hasn't been so long. An hour perhaps," said Max, smiling down at her. "I am glad you could get away."

"I had a fitting, and . . . oh, how I despise London and all of the constraints it puts on me," said Kate, her green eyes

136

flashing with defiance.

"But I thought the objective of all young ladies was to come to London and find the man of their dreams," said Max. "It never occurred to me, I suppose, that anyone would not like it here."

"Most young ladies are like that, I suppose, but I am not in the least excited by the prospect of balls and such. What I really want is to get my hands on enough money to go back home with my mare and live in peace."

Kate watched his face as he digested this information. She tried to ignore the niggling hope that his expression would register disappointment — disappointment that she might not want to become a part of his world.

His eyes, however, showed only puzzlement, and he said, "The mare your father is selling to finance the Season you did not even want."

Her chin held high, Kate said, "Yes, that's the one. Ironic, is it not?"

He smiled again, his blue eyes twinkling. "Then you will be delighted when I tell you that I have come up with a plan."

"You have?" she exclaimed with a little squeal before shushing herself and leaning closer to him.

"Certainly. I know what it is like to have no money, to have to sell the thing that you love. We are friends, are we not, Kate? I want to help you. I mean, my own future and happiness will soon be secure. I want to do what I can to secure yours."

Kate smiled up at him. How could she not? He had no idea that her feelings for him had changed, but he still wanted to help her. He really was like Sir Milton.

"What is your plan, Mr. Darby?" she asked eagerly.

"We have had the means all along," he said.

"What are you talking about?"

"Don't you see? Thunderlight. You can race him again. There are always young men up from the country who think they have a chance to beat him. Men who rate their own mounts and horsemanship too highly."

"But, Max, I cannot do that! What would happen when Papa found out? And you know he would! And then Mama would learn of it and become upset. I would be ruined — not that I care, but Mama does. I simply cannot do it," she said dolefully, not even realizing she had called him by his given name.

In return, Max said, "Not you, Kate . . . me!"

He sat back, his arms folded across his chest, supremely confident that he had saved the day. Kate frowned a moment and then her face cleared, a growing smile on her lips.

"Oh, Max! How clever of you! Papa and Mama may learn of it and be angry, but they cannot accuse me of ruining my reputation. It is the perfect scheme!" said Kate, throwing her arms around his neck.

Then his lips met hers, and Kate felt a jolt of excitement course through her veins. In amazement, she kissed him back. After a moment, she withdrew her arms, and he lifted his head, grinning at her from ear to ear.

Kate sat back, her own eyes glowing with some undefined emotion. She quickly looked away, though she knew he had not noticed. She could tell from his fervent gaze that he was already picturing himself riding Thunderlight to victory.

"When and how?" she asked in a detached tone.

"Ah, leave that to me, my dear. I will take care of everything. I will send you word tomorrow. Now, you had better go. Wouldn't do for your parents to discover you here with me. Not yet."

Kate rose and went to the gate, pausing

to look back at him. He had already forgotten his shocking kiss and was completely oblivious to its effect on her.

So much for Max Darby being her Sir Milton, her shining knight.

Five

Kate was in a better frame of mind by that evening when she was dressing for the theater. Maxwell Darby might not be her ideal knight, but he had devised a method for her to keep her beloved Early Girl. It was not foolproof, but it was as close to a sure thing as she had ever seen.

And while Max might hold a certain fascination for her, she prided herself on her practicality. First things first. Let him win another horse for her father to sell at auction. Then she would see if there was a reason to hope for more.

Kate grinned at her image, causing Dolly, who was arranging her red curls, to smile and tease, "You have a bloom in your cheeks, Miss Kate. You must be thinking of some young man."

"Nonsense, it is simply hot in here. That is why I am flushed. Why do you not open a window?" asked Kate, fanning her face with her hand.

"Window or no, miss, you cannot put anything past old Dolly."

"Nonsense," said Kate, but she grinned at the maid.

Just then the door opened and her mother, dressed in a pale lilac evening gown, entered the room.

"Oh, you look beautiful, Mama."

"A right treat for the eyes, madam," agreed the maid.

"You are too kind," she said, floating into the room and sitting on Kate's bed so that her image was in the dressing mirror.

"Did you want something, Mama?" asked Kate after watching her mother mutilate a lace handkerchief.

"Yes, I . . . oh, it is so unpleasant, but you know that I called on your aunt this afternoon, after meeting our neighbor." Her mother's gaze met hers in the mirror.

Kate looked away. Her mother could never get to the point when she had something unpleasant to relate.

"How is Auntie?"

"She is fine, dear. I asked her about the status of our neighbors, the Darby brothers."

"Oh, what sort of status?" asked Kate, twisting one curl around her ear and pretending not to be interested in the least.

"You know, whether or not they are suitable."

"And what did she tell you? Not that I care," she added.

"That they are suitable as far as lineage, but, my dear, they are shockingly poor. Perhaps poorer than we are. I mean, we at least have land and horses. They have nothing except their good names."

"Oh, I see," said Kate, unable to keep the disappointment out of her voice.

Her mother rose and came to stand behind her, placing a sympathetic hand on her shoulder. "I thought you should know."

Kate managed a brave smile and said, "I really had not begun to think about Mr. Darby in those terms, Mama. Really, I had not."

"I'm glad. I knew you would be sensible," said Mrs. O'Connor, patting the slender shoulder. "I also wanted to warn you that, before you came down this afternoon, Mr. Darby did mention that he was interested in Philippa Beauchamp. After finding out about his lack of funds, I understand why."

"Of course. One cannot blame him for trying to better himself through marriage. Is it not what you want for me?" asked Kate with a glittery smile that failed to bring that telltale animation to her emerald eyes.

"For you, my dear child, I want happiness, only happiness." Mrs. O'Connor gave her shoulder a last squeeze and glided toward the door. There, she said, "Do hurry, Kate. You know how your father hates to be late to the theater. He wants to have plenty of time to settle in for his nap."

"I will be down in five minutes, Mama."

The maid gave her hair a final touch and pronounced her finished. With a smile, Kate dismissed her.

Alone, Kate had the most immoderate desire to tear at her hair and throw herself across the bed in tears. She chided herself for the emotion. How could she possibly have thought that Mr. Darby had any interest in her — any romantic interest? Had he shown her that he did, beyond their lighthearted banter as Sir Milton and Iseult? Certainly not. He had been a perfect gentleman and was even offering to help her out of her difficulty. He did not deserve anger or tears. He had not betrayed her in any way.

Kate rose and walked to the window, her willowy frame draped to perfection by her elegant blue silk gown. Her steps were regal, and she held her chin high. At the window, she gazed into the garden, staring at the wall where she knew the shrubbery hid the old gate.

No, Max Darby had not betrayed her. Her heart had done that, without her even knowing it was happening.

Kate smiled as her father winked at her and then leaned closer to her mother, saying, "You will put all the young ladies to shame tonight, my dear."

"Whatever do you mean, Kieran?"

"What do I mean?" he asked. "Why, with that pretty gown and that golden hair of yours, every man's eye will be on you, my love."

Her mother gurgled with laughter and slapped him playfully with her fan. "Gold with gray streaks," she said.

"Gold and silver, my dear. There is nothing a man likes more than gold and silver."

Kate turned and looked out the window as the carriage carried them to Covent Garden and the theater. She knew that Max would be there, and she was gathering her fortitude to withstand the onslaught of her own emotions when she saw him. It was a shame that he was poor and that he was interested in someone who was not. But her mother's speech had sealed her fate, and she knew it did not lie with Max Darby.

When they entered the lobby of the theater, her aunt and uncle were waiting for them. Her uncle, Lord Murray, took her mother's arm, trailing along after her father and her aunt. At the last minute, her uncle turned and offered his other arm to her, saving her from walking behind them like a child.

The gas lights flickered in their sconces, highlighting the beautiful fabrics of the ladies' gowns as they passed through to their box. Kate had been to the theater only once before, and she was looking forward to it.

As if he had read her thoughts, her uncle said, "Are you looking forward to the play tonight, my dear?"

"Oh yes."

"So you are fond of the theater?"

"Yes, uncle, I think it would be wonderful to act on the stage. Only think of all the roles one could play."

"True, but afterward, one would have to leave off the role of queen or knight and return to the mundane world. That might prove quite trying, puss," he said.

Kate laughed, tossing her head at his witticism. Raising her eyes again, she saw him. He was striding toward them, his handsome face eager. His brother followed more slowly.

She must have tensed, for her uncle asked, "What is it?"

"Nothing, only someone we know."

"Mr. Darby, how nice to see you again so soon," said her mother, nodding to his bow. "Allow me to present my sister's husband, Lord Murray. Alfred, this is Maxwell Darby."

"How do you do, my lord? Good evening, Miss O'Connor."

"Mr. Darby," said Kate, quite proud of herself for her polite tone.

"Allow me to present my brother Tristram. Tris, this is Lord Murray, Mrs. O'Connor, and Miss O'Connor. The ladies are our neighbors."

"How do you do?" said the young man, sweeping an elegant bow.

Kate curtsied in reply, marveling at the resemblance between the brothers. She had been too upset that afternoon to notice. Tristram was every bit as handsome as his older brother, but his blond hair and pale blue eyes made him a watercolor image of the darker Max.

They continued on their way to the boxes, and Kate found herself by Max's side.

"I have already put out feelers for our

match race. I think Palmer may take the bait."

"Excellent," she whispered, quite pleased with the normality of her tone.

"Perhaps we should meet tomorrow morning, in the park. I would certainly feel better if I could put Thunderlight through his paces again."

"What a good idea," she said. "At nine o'clock?"

"At the entrance to the park. I will be there. Ah, here we are, Tris. Delightful to meet you, my lord," said Max, sketching a bow to them before leading his brother away.

"Pleasant young men, though the dark one, Max, has something of a reputation," said her uncle, watching Kate keenly.

"What sort of reputation?"

"A bit of a daredevil, so they say. Of course, he could not be much different from your papa in his day," added her uncle.

"Papa had a reputation?" asked Kate, loudly enough for her father, who had come looking for them, to protest.

"Completely undeserved," he said. "And I'll thank you, Alfred, not to be disparaging me in front of my own daughter."

"Never disparaging, Kieran, just taking

off some of that polish."

Kate entered the box and took the seat beside her mother. Her aunt and mother were already busy discussing the parade of fashions in the opposite boxes. She was glad, for it gave her time to search for Max Darby.

She had no trouble spotting them as the brothers made their entrance into the Beauchamp box, since Mrs. Beauchamp exclaimed loudly, "Mr. Darby, do come and sit right here beside me. Do move over, Philippa."

Kate's sharp eyes detected his expression of distaste as he allowed the vulgar Mrs. Beauchamp to drag him into the seat next to hers. His smile appeared forced, but he did not draw away from her.

Kate's attention was diverted by a cackle from the box next to theirs. She cocked her head to one side to better hear the masculine voices.

"There they are, Tavistoke. I told you, this is going to be better than the play. Look, the woman's practically throwing herself at him."

"I told you my boys would not let us down, Cravenwell. Max will have the Beauchamp girl all sewed up within the week. Just watch and see."

Kate closed her eyes and swallowed. It was just as bad as she had thought. Max was nothing but the basest fortune hunter. Even his father, Lord Tavistoke, knew about it and was egging him on. Was the entire family devoid of honor?

"Heh, heh. Look at her now. Giving him a real show. Too bad her weasel of a husband is in the back of the box. Puts a bit of a damper on the show," said Cravenwell.

"Not too much," said Tavistoke with a crude laugh. "She's put her hand on his knee. Watch out, my boy! Don't let the creature go too far!"

The next four hours were a pantomime of torture for Kate as she watched Mrs. Beauchamp flirt outrageously with Max Darby, their actions crudely narrated by the two men in the adjoining box. For his part, Max seemed willing to withstand everything she could serve up, despite the fact that Mr. Beauchamp remained in the box until the second interval. Sitting at the back of the box, he had a clear view of all his wife's shocking posturing.

It would have been amusing if it had been anyone else, but for Kate, watching Max's efforts to ingratiate himself with the mother made her ill. When the intervals came, other men arrived in the Beauchamp box to leer at Miss Beauchamp and bow over the vulgar mother's hand — men equally desperate, she supposed, to gain a fortune. In all of this, the husband never moved, never reacted.

By the time her mother and aunt rose at the end of the final act, Kate felt numb. All the way home, all she could think of was Max and that woman. Or worse yet, Max and that insipid girl. Not insipid. She had appeared to be enjoying Tristram's earnest conversation.

Kate suddenly realized any regard she had been harboring for Max Darby was dead. How could she possibly respect someone so sunk to good taste and decorum?

When she finally reached the sanctity of her room and laid her head on her pillow, she sighed at the touch of the cool, soft cotton on her heated cheek. There were no tears, only sadness at what might have been.

Kate comforted herself with the thought that any man she chose would have to put honor before fortune — even if he were a beggar. Max had chosen fortune.

No, Max Darby was not the man for her.

The next morning, clouds covered the

sky as well as Kate's spirit. She had settled the matter of Max Darby in her mind, but her heart was having trouble being converted. She knew she should give up on him, but a part of her, the part that wanted to shake him until his teeth rattled, wanted to rescue him from this awful situation. She was torn between disgust and attraction, despair and hope.

Hope won out, and she dressed in her dark green habit and sent for her groom and Thunderlight. She would meet Max in the park. She would accept his help in her efforts to keep her father from selling Early Girl.

Entering the park, she could not help but smile. Max sat astride the big gray gelding, his seat perfection as he watched her approach. He was the consummate horseman, communicating by silent commands with his mount.

"You look lovely this morning," he said.

Kate frowned slightly, and then said, "Oh, I thought you were speaking to Thunderlight."

"No you did not," said Max, bringing the gray closer until his thigh touched hers.

"Very well," she said, her breathing erratic. "Thank you, Mr. Darby. May I say you look quite dashing, too."

He chuckled, and Kate found herself relaxing again. This was the Max she knew, the Max from the garden.

Leaning closer, he whispered, "Can we talk in front of . . ."

He nodded to her groom and Kate said, "Yes, Bobby knows what we are about. He does not like it, but he will keep it to himself. Will you not, Bobby?"

"Aye, miss, that I will. Else Mr. MacAfee will have my heart for breakfast. If it were anyone else goin' t' ride the big stallion, I woulda tried t' talk the mistress out of it. But I remember you from before, I do. If anyone can win the race, you can, Mr. Darby. An' then Mr. O'Connor, 'e won't hafta sell Early Girl."

"Early Girl has been in Bobby's charge since she was foaled," confided Kate.

"I see. Well, I appreciate your confidence, Bobby. I shan't let you down, any of you."

The groom nodded and kicked his pony, guiding him away from them. Max slid to the ground and turned to help Kate dismount. The saddles were soon switched, and Kate allowed Max to throw her into the saddle before he climbed onto Thunderlight.

"Palmer has taken the bait," he said.

"What is his horse like?"

"I don't know," said Max, grinning when her eyes grew wide. "I know Palmer's sort. He'll have a showy, prime piece of blood, but when it comes down to it, he won't have the faintest idea how to get the best out of his horse. But don't worry, I have sent Needham, Lord Cravenwell's groom, to find out all he can about the horse."

"When is the race?"

"Tomorrow morning. It will be a near run thing, I can tell you."

"Oh, Max, I hope . . ."

He placed a finger against her lips before winking at her and giving her another of his warm smiles. He was so handsome, she thought. If only . . .

"Do not worry. I will not fail you. And in the afternoon, when your father is getting ready to take your mare to Tattersall's, you will calmly present him with Palmer's horse as a substitute."

"He will be so angry," she said. Then, with a giggle, she added, "Mostly, he will be angry that he did not think of it himself."

"And that he missed the race."

"There is that, too," she said, and they shared a laugh.

154

"Well, no time like the present to put the old boy through his paces. Will you ride with me?"

"You know I will," said Kate. "Bobby, give us a signal, will you?"

The groom nodded, took his handkerchief out of his pocket and held it in the air. "Ready . . . steady . . . go!" he shouted, letting the handkerchief flutter to the ground.

Thunderlight leaped ahead, but the big gray soon caught up. The two huge horses careened through the park, their hooves churning up the turf. Kate watched as Thunderlight slowly edged ahead. She marveled as the gray began to tire, but Thunderlight continued on, as strong as ever.

When she finally reached their starting point, Max was already there, cooling Thunderlight by walking him in a wide circle.

Joining him, she said, "He is the fastest horse I have ever seen — at least, when you are riding him. He really wants to please you."

"And he does," said Max, leaning over the big stallion's arched neck and patting him fiercely.

Kate felt her heart catch in her throat.

She fought the urge to shout at him, to demand that he cease all the nonsense about courting Philippa Beauchamp. Max Darby was perfect, but not for such a retiring little chit. He was perfect for her — Kate O'Connor! Why could he not see it?

"Is something wrong? No, no, don't tell me. You are still worried about tomorrow. We will win, Kate. Trust me."

He put one hand over hers and gave a squeeze. Kate gazed down at the strong, leather-clad fingers and wished with all her heart she could tell him what she was really thinking. She could not, of course. For one thing, he would be shocked. She was certain he had no idea what wild emotions he had stirred in her heart. And secondly, he had given her no indication that he might share those sentiments. No, she would have to keep her thoughts and emotions to herself.

She lifted her eyes and smiled at him. "I do trust you, Max. As a matter of fact, I am placing all my trust in you."

"I will not let you down," he said, bringing her gloved hand to his lips and kissing it.

With a jaunty grin, he released her hand and slid to the ground. Taking her by the waist, he took her off the gray as if she weighed no more than a feather. When she was on her feet, she looked up at him, the smile freezing on her lips.

With the horses on either side of them, he pulled her close and kissed her mouth — a deep, searching kiss that made her forget all her good resolutions.

Then he released her, and the horses moved apart. Without a word, he signaled her groom, and they quickly switched the saddles back. Max threw her onto Thunderlight's back before swinging onto the big gray gelding.

"At eight o'clock tomorrow morning, Bobby. See that you have your mistress here, with Thunderlight, on time."

"Aye, guvner," said the groom.

"Good-bye, Kate. Until tomorrow morning."

And he was gone before she could say a word. Not that she was capable of speech at the moment. That kiss had absolutely shocked her — and warmed her from the tip of her toes to the top of her head. She had received a number of kisses, but never one as earth-shattering as Max's — or as disturbing.

"So much for my good, sensible intentions," she muttered under her breath as she turned Thunderlight for home.

"Wot was that, miss?" asked the groom.

"Nothing, Bobby, nothing at all. Just remember what Mr. Darby said. I shan't send to the stables, for it might arouse suspicion. Instead, tell Mr. MacAfee that I am joining a group of friends for an early ride. He will not question that."

The groom looked incredulous at this, and Kate grimaced. "Oh, just tell him. The only way he can question it is by coming to the house and asking me, and he will not dare do that so early in the morning."

"Yes, miss," said the groom. After a moment, he asked, "This isn't something we're goin' t' be doin' on a regular basis, is it, miss?"

"No, Bobby. This is a one time thing. After tomorrow, it will all be over."

"I hope so, miss. I surely do hope so."

"So do I," whispered Kate.

After returning his horse to the Marquess of Cravenwell's mews, Max walked back to the small town house he and his brother shared. With a distracted greeting for their servant, he made his way to his room and pulled off his boots.

He was restless, though he did not go so far as to question his plan to win another horse for Kieran O'Connor. He was certain he and Thunderlight would win. As for Kate . . .

Max rose and took a quick turn around the small room. He picked up his boots and placed them in the cupboard. Then he took them out again.

"Barton!"

"Yes, sir," said the servant, appearing immediately.

"These need shining," he said, pointing at the boots.

"Indeed yes," said the servant, hurrying across the room and gathering the boots to his chest. "Is there anything else?"

"No, not now."

"Very good, sir," said Barton, backing out of the room.

Max removed his snugly fitted coat and waistcoat, throwing them over the small chair. He caught a glimpse of his reflection in the mirror over the mantel. He was frowning fiercely. With an effort, he relaxed his expression, but his image reflected his uneasiness.

"Bah!" he said, flopping down on the chair. "Kate, what the devil have you done to me? All I wanted was a light flirtation . . ."

He groaned in frustration. A light flirtation with her while courting Philippa Beauchamp. It was working out just as he had planned. So why did he feel so bad?

Kate was hardly a child. She knew how things were between them, and he had made no secret of the fact that he planned to wed Philippa.

Ah, but the passion he had felt in that kiss! That was what troubled him. Max tore his cravat from his neck and cursed.

Women! They were more trouble than they were worth! No wonder he preferred horses!

"Max, that you?" asked Tristram, opening the door and poking his head through.

"Yes, it's me. What do you want?"

"Whoa. Nothing, brother. I just wondered if I should come in and wish you happy. You had mentioned last night, after the theater, that you thought you might speak to Philippa's father today."

"What? Oh, yes. Sorry, Tris. No, I haven't gotten around to that yet. I was just going to get cleaned up and change."

"I . . . I see. Max, are you sure about this? I mean, do you really want to marry Miss Beauchamp?"

"Want to? What has that to say in the matter? I have no choice. One of us has to wed money, if not both, and I don't see you rushing about looking for a likely prospect."

"Well, no, I haven't. I have been a little preoccupied, finishing the next book and all. You're right. I shouldn't question you when I have done nothing to help out. Sorry."

Max rose and smiled at his brother, saying, "No, I shouldn't have spoken so. And you have helped out. You have spent hours telling Miss Beauchamp what a wonderful chap I am, have you not?"

"Uh, yes, that's true."

"Then do not worry about it, Tris. I shall marry the heiress, and you will reap the reward, too. That's how we Darbys handle things, right?"

"Precisely," said Tristram. He pushed his blond hair off his forehead and opened his mouth. Then he shook his head and said, "So you are going in a few minutes."

"Yes, as soon as I rid myself of the smell of the stables."

"Oh, that's where you have been," said Tristram. "Trying out Thunderlight with Miss O'Connor?"

"Yes. She is quite a horsewoman, you know. She rode the big gray and nearly kept up with us all around the park. I was very impressed."

"Funny, isn't it?"

"What?" said Max, removing his cambric shirt.

"Well, I mean, there you are with Miss O'Connor, who loves her horses as much as you do, and . . ."

"What? Are you saying I should be asking for Kate instead of Philippa?"

"No, I . . ."

"Well, if, as Monsieur Pangloss told Candide, this were the best of all possible worlds, then perhaps that is how things would turn up, but this is . . . oh, blast! Barton! Where are my clean shirts?" shouted Max.

Tristram chuckled. "This is quite a day for you, Max. Here you are, quoting Voltaire, and I am advocating that you and the horse-mad Miss O'Connor are quite well suited. I believe we have had a shift in the universe. At the very least, our world is slipping on its axis."

"What are you talking about, Tristram? Ah, there you are, Barton. Where are my shirts?"

"I put them in the top drawer, Master Max. See, right where they always are. You must have looked in the wrong one. Let me," said the servant, taking out a shirt and helping Max put it on.

Max turned to his brother and said, "Look, Tristram. I am going to see Mr. Beauchamp, and hopefully by the end of

162

the day, I will have secured my heiress. Why don't you get out of this house and see if you can manage to meet someone, too? Leave it, Barton. I can tie my own cravat, remember?"

"Very good, sir. Shall you be wearing the bottle green coat?"

"If you will just step this way, sir."

Max followed the butler along the wide marble hall, turning down a short corridor until he was ushered into a spacious library.

"Come in, Mr. Darby," said the little man behind the huge desk. "Won't you have a seat on the sofa? I will be with you in a moment. I am in the middle of something."

Max did as he was bid and sat down. All four walls were covered with books, from floor to ceiling. A huge rolling ladder was attached to one of these walls. Several narrow tables were scattered about the room, each containing stacks of books. Max thought to himself that this would be Tristram's idea of heaven.

The butler, who had followed him inside, said, "Would you care for something to drink, sir? Mr. Beauchamp has a very good port, and the brandy . . ."

"Try the port, Mr. Darby. You can never go wrong with a stout port," said the figure behind the desk.

"The port will be fine," said Max.

After handing him the glass, the butler withdrew. Max sipped the ruby liquid and continued to watch his host surreptitiously.

Finally, with an audible sigh, the little man closed the ledger he was poring over and rose. Without speaking, he went to the table with the decanters and poured himself a large glass. He waved the decanter at Max in question.

Max shook his head and waited while the other man joined him on the sofa.

"Now, young man, what did you wish to see me about today?"

"I shall get straight to the point, sir. I am interested in your daughter."

"My daughter? I see. I find that rather amusing, sir. Last night at the theater, I would have guessed that you were interested in my wife."

This was delivered with a wheezing gasp that Max supposed passed for laughter.

"While I may admire your good wife, Mr. Beauchamp, it is your daughter who has gained my complete attention."

"Humph. I see. What color are her eyes?"

"Her eyes?" asked Max. "Why, they are as blue as the ocean."

"Actually, the ocean is usually more gray than blue, my boy, but you would not know that since you probably spend a great deal more time studying horses and women than you do books."

Max stiffened. "I assure you, sir, I have not been . . ."

"There, there," soothed the small man. "I did not mean any insult. Very few people spend as much time with books as I do. So you want to marry my sweet Philippa. She is nothing like her mother, you know."

"I . . . I did guess that, sir."

"And you do not mind?"

Max thought privately that if Philippa were anything like her mother, he would not be where he was at that very moment. Philippa's being the direct opposite of her mother was the most pleasing of her attributes.

"Not at all," he said quickly.

"Good, that's good. Are you aware that Philippa has an inheritance of her own, deliverable on her marriage?"

"No, sir, I was not."

"So you only hoped that I would settle enough money on her to fix up that sad little bit of land."

"There is a house on the property," said Max, forgetting to question how Beauchamp could possibly know about his own prospects.

"A house? A shack, more like, but that is neither here nor there. No, you need not worry about that scrap of property. I will gladly settle a fine estate and ample funds on the man who weds my little girl. However, you must win not only my approval and my wife's, but also my daughter's. Come back next week after you have done what you can to please my daughter. Then we will speak of this matter again."

"I . . . I don't understand, Mr. Beauchamp," said Max.

"You must make Philippa want to marry you, Mr. Darby. It is as simple as that. If you succeed, then you shall have my blessing, as well as my wife's."

He rose and returned to his vast desk. Max stood and walked to the door.

"I will do so, sir. May I take her driving this afternoon?"

"That is the trick, is it not? Managing to take Philippa for a drive without her mother's interference. I wish you luck, Mr. Darby."

"Thank you, sir," said Max, turning the handle.

"Oh, and Mr. Darby."

"Yes, sir?"

"Make no mistake about it. My wife may be as vulgar as everyone says, but she loves her daughter and will settle for nothing but the best for her. If you wish to marry Philippa, you must be the best. Good day."

"Good day, sir," said Max, frowning as he made his way back to the front hall. When he arrived there, he asked the starchy butler, "Is Miss Beauchamp at home?"

"I shall ascertain, sir."

Max stood there, slapping his leather gloves against his thigh. Suddenly, he heard a familiar laugh, and he shrank against the wall. The last person he wanted to see at that moment was Miss Beauchamp's ill-mannered mother.

"I'm telling you, my girl, that this is just the sort of man . . . oh, Mr. Darby, how good of you to call," said Mrs. Beauchamp, dragging her daughter along and thrusting her forward. The scarlet-faced girl ducked her head.

"Good afternoon, Mrs. Beauchamp and Miss Beauchamp. I had called to see if I might take Miss Beauchamp for a drive in the park. The day is a little chilly, but it is still dry."

"Of course Philippa would like to go for a drive with you, my dear young man!" She added coyly, "I know you would like for me to go with you, too, but I am afraid my husband has requested my help in a family matter."

"That is too bad," said Max, trying not to smile too brightly at this bit of news. "Another time."

"Oh yes, another time. Now, you two run along. And, Philippa, remember what I was saying."

The girl by his side emitted an incoherent sound, which he took for assent. Max offered his arm, leading her outside to the waiting carriage.

Max had chosen the marquess's phaeton. It was a sleek carriage pulled by a pair of matched bays with gaits as smooth as glass. They were a joy to drive, and Max knew how to drive to an inch. They leaped forward, causing the girl by his side to emit another little squeak.

"If you do not mind, Miss Beauchamp, I will keep my mind on my cattle until we arrive in the park." After this, Max was silent as he expertly guided his horses through the heavy afternoon traffic. As he passed a wagon carrying produce from the country, he found himself facing down a heavy traveling carriage. With a gentle tug, he had the phaeton out of harm's way, but not before the girl squeaked once more.

"Really, Miss Beauchamp, I am accounted a very competent whip. You need not fear that I will upset us," he reassured. When her grip on the side of the seat did not abate, he added testily, "Perhaps you would prefer to drive."

She lifted her head and fixed him with a wide-eyed stare of horror. Immediately, he felt contrite.

"I beg your pardon, Miss Beauchamp . . . Philippa. I did not mean to frighten you." She resumed her previous position, looking at her lap.

Max shook his head. Well, he supposed he should have guessed that it would take some work before his intended learned to trust him. She was very shy, and he would have to give her time.

All at once, Max recalled riding in the carriage with Philippa and her mother. Tristram and Philippa had practically had their heads together, chatting easily with each other. It was difficult to reconcile this image with the silent girl by his side. Yes, he definitely had his work cut out for him.

He turned the phaeton into the park, which was teeming with people, some in carriages and some on horseback, as well as the occasional pedestrians. It was as if everyone knew the days of fair weather were numbered and wanted to take advantage of this ritual opportunity to see and be seen.

"It is very crowded today," he said.

"Yes," said Miss Beauchamp.

"It is very pleasant, however, to know that I am escorting the prettiest girl here." Instead of the expected smile, his comment earned him only a quick glance, followed by her tucking her chin against her chest so that he could not even see her profile. With a grimace, Max redoubled his efforts.

"That is the most fetching bonnet you are wearing, Miss Beauchamp."

"Thank you," she whispered.

"Of course, it cannot compare to your face."

No response.

"A face I would dearly love to see," said Max dryly.

She seemed to consider his words and lifted her face briefly before turning away.

Max frowned. He would very much have liked to ask her what game she was playing. Surely that was not fear he had read in her eyes. Or aversion, for that matter. The girl hardly knew him, except through what Tristram had told her about him. And he refused to believe Tristram would have betrayed him.

Just then, he heard his father calling his name, and he pulled up beside a passing landaulet which contained the gregarious Lady Anne and his father.

"Well met," said the viscount, detaching Lady Anne's arm from his. "Allow me to present you to Lady Anne Graves. This is my son Maxwell."

"How do you do, my lady? Are you acquainted with Miss Beauchamp?"

The introductions were followed by general pronouncements on the fine weather they were enjoying, and Max was ready to move along. His father, however, appeared loath to part.

"So, my boy, is this the young lady you cannot say enough about?"

"Really, Papa, you must not . . ."

"Oh, I'm sure Miss Beauchamp does not mind. Do you, my dear?"

The young lady at his side murmured something unintelligible, and Lady Anne responded, "It don't pay to be so missish, child. Otherwise, you'll end up like me, and money ain't everything."

"We really should move along. We are

blocking too many people," said Max hastily. "A pleasure meeting you, Lady Anne." With a flick of his whip, he sent his team ahead.

After another fifteen minutes of silence, Max said, "Miss Beauchamp, have I done something to offend you?"

She shook her head.

"Then why have you taken me in dislike? I must tell you, I find your attitude very unsettling."

"I do . . . not . . . dislike you, Mr. Darby. I do not know you."

Max relaxed. Bashfulness was indeed a terrible thing, but he was confident that he would be able to win her over. She just needed a chance to get to know him better.

"I am very glad to hear it, Miss Beauchamp, because I must tell you that I have spoken to your father."

This time, her eyes fairly flew to his face, and he clearly read dismay. Controlling his impatience, he gave her one of his winning smiles — a smile that had won the heart of many a maid.

"But I told you that I do not know you, sir."

He chuckled and said, "But you will get to know me, my dear. That is what this is all about, is it not? You will get to know me, and then . . . but we have time, my dear Miss Beauchamp. We have plenty of time."

At this, she sagged against him, insensible to any more of his winning smiles or words.

"Blast!" said Max, transferring the ribbons to one hand and propping her up against him with the other. As he turned the carriage, the thought passed through his mind that she would have been very impressed with his driving had she only been conscious.

Six

"She did what?"

"She fainted," said Max.

"What the devil did you say to her?" demanded Tristram, leaping to his feet and striding the length of the room to stand in front of his brother, glaring ferociously.

"All I said was that I had spoken to her father."

"You must have said or done something else to alarm her, to frighten her!" exclaimed Tristram, marching back the way he had just come.

"I assure you, I said nothing upsetting. Oh, I complimented her bonnet and made some absurd comment about being with the prettiest girl in the park." While his brother continued his pacing, Max sat on the sofa with his arms crossed, a thoughtful frown on his face. "I tell you, Tris, it is enough to make me doubt my abilities with the ladies."

Tristram stopped and said softly, "Perhaps you should — at least with this particular young lady."

Ignoring this, Max suddenly snapped his

fingers. "No, I will view it as a challenge. I already know that the mother would not mind having me around, and the father did not turn me down completely. No, I must simply press my suit with Miss Beauchamp. I shall start by sending her flowers. Lilacs, I think."

"Not lilacs. It should be daisies," muttered Tris.

"Daisies? Very well. Barton!" roared Max, bringing the servant scurrying into the room.

"I want to send Miss Beauchamp some daisies. How does a fellow go about doing that?"

"I can take care of that for you, Master Max. If you will write a card, I will take it along with me."

"A card?" said Max, grimacing at the thought. "I am not the poet. You'll do it for me, won't you, Tris? Something sweet, but not too flowery, or Miss Beauchamp will never believe it was written by me."

Tristram looked mulish, but he sat down at the small desk and dipped his pen in the inkwell.

After a moment, Max asked impatiently, "Well, can't you think of anything?"

"Do not rush me, Max." With a bold stroke, he began. After five minutes, he sanded the paper and handed it to Max.

"Humph, a little flowery, but not too bad. Listen to this, Barton."

Your hair, those eyes, that smile and nose,
Nothing can compare to the beauty
each of these possess.
And yet the whole wins any contest
In my heart.

"Yes, that should do. Thank you, Tris. Now, I'll just sign it, and Barton can be on his way." Taking the pen, Max frowned. Then, with a nod, he added: *Your obedient servant, Max Darby.*

"That should do the trick."

"Very good, Master Max. Now, I shall just take this along with me."

"Don't forget, Barton. It has to be daisies," called Max.

Rubbing his hands together, Max turned to speak to his brother, but Tristram had disappeared. With a shrug, he moved to the tray of decanters and filled a large glass.

Moving Tristram's sketchbook, he sat down on the sofa. As he sipped the golden liquid, he flipped through the pages, struck once again by the scope of his younger brother's artistic talent. These were no mere scribbles. They were worthy of publication.

Max's smile widened as he came across Tristram's interpretation of him, dressed as a knight of old. Tristram had labeled it *Sir Milton*. He turned another page and found the drawing of a lady in a cone-shaped hat and flowing gown. With the label of *Iseult*, he gazed at the woman's face for a moment before realizing it was not Kate, whom Tristram had nicknamed Iseult, but Philippa Beauchamp. Odd, thought Max, turning another page.

"May I have that back?" asked Tristram, standing over Max and holding out his hand.

"Certainly," he said, closing the book and handing it to his brother. "I hope you do not think I was prying. I picked it up to move it, and I opened it. I had forgotten how talented you are, Tris."

"Thank you," said Tristram stiffly. He turned and walked away.

Max was about to call him back, but his stomach growled, and he went in search of food instead. The cook, who came in during the day, was busily preparing their dinner. She greeted Max with a curtsy when he entered the kitchen.

"Good afternoon, Mrs. Owens."

"Good afternoon, sir."

"I am sorry to invade your kitchen, but I sent Barton out on an errand and now find that I am feeling quite ravenous. You wouldn't have a little something that could tide me over until tonight, would you?" He smiled at her, and she was putty in his hands.

"Oh, yes, sir," she said, heading toward the larder. "Just give me a moment to fix you a tray. Shall I bring it to the drawing room?"

"Yes, please. Thank you," said Max, strolling back the way he had come.

"My pleasure, Mr. Darby," called the cook.

"You will marry the man, Philippa, whether you love him or not. Whoever has been planting these strange notions in your head? Marriage is not about love," said Mrs. Beauchamp, sparing a look of derision for her husband.

"Papa!" cried Philippa.

"Child, I know that you are not well acquainted with Mr. Darby, but he is the first to offer for you since . . . since that incident last spring. I think we would be foolish to turn down the chance to see you settled. I mean, he is presentable enough,

178

is he not?" asked Mr. Beauchamp.

"He is handsome in the extreme!" said his wife.

"And he is young and fit."

"Very fit," added his wife.

"He seems very kind, too," said her father.

"The essence of kindness, Philippa. Pray stop that caterwauling," said Mrs. Beauchamp, glaring at her daughter. Philippa's sobs subsided, but she continued to sniffle.

"Oh, I have done with her, Mr. Beauchamp!" said her mother before she flounced out of the room.

"Philippa, you do wish to wed, do you not?" said her father, handing her his handkerchief to replace the scrap of lace she was using.

"Yes, Papa."

"Then I think we must face the fact that after that fiasco last spring, we are out of options. Mr. Darby is the only man to come up to scratch since your mother . . . no, I cannot bear to repeat the story, but I know what it has cost you, losing your vouchers to Almack's. And the invitations are fewer this fall. I am afraid your status in Society has changed irrevocably."

"I wonder why," said Philippa with unaccustomed sarcasm. "Throwing herself at the husband of one of Almack's hostesses, and in the middle of Almack's, no less. Oh, Papa, how can you put up with it?"

"I know," said the diminutive man, sitting down next to her on the sofa. "You must think me the perfect fool."

"Oh, no, Papa! Never that!" she said, taking his hand and squeezing it.

"You should, because I am a fool," he said, looking her in the eye. "But my reason, despite all your mother says and does, all she has ever said or done, is love. I have always loved her, and I always will."

"Papa, why don't you . . ." Philippa sighed. It would do no good to lecture her father on his meekness. He was a clever businessman, but he was nothing more than a mouse around her overbearing mother.

"So will you accept Mr. Darby? You need not live near your mother, you know. I will settle a handsome sum on you. You and he may have an estate wherever you wish. Only say the word, my dear."

Philippa looked at her father's hopeful face, closed her eyes, and nodded.

"When he asks me, I shall accept."

Max's afternoon and evening were quiet.

Tristram had disappeared, as he often did, leaving Max to dine alone. It did not bother him. He had planned an early night in order to be well rested for the race the next morning.

After playing patience for an hour, he set aside the cards and wandered to his room. There, he stripped off his clothes and threw himself onto the bed. Two hours later, the clock struck midnight.

"Blast," he muttered, rolling off the soft feather mattress and rising. He pulled on his unmentionables and a dressing gown and left the room, in search of company and diversion.

Tristram was still gone, so he was out of luck.

Suddenly he smiled. "Midnight!"

The happy thought that Kate might be outside in her garden, unable to sleep just like him, led him to the garden wall.

"Kate! Kate, are you there?"

He pushed the gate open and whispered, "Kate?"

"I'm here," she replied, her white wrapper looming suddenly in front of him.

"Thank heavens," he said, extending his hand and leading her back to his side of the garden wall. "We can be sure of our privacy on this side of the wall."

"I cannot stay long," she said softly. "I could not sleep, and I came outside on the chance that you would be here."

"It was much the same for me," Max replied, seating her on the stone bench before joining her there. She shivered, and he put an arm around her, saying, "Just to keep you warm, my dear."

"I know."

They sat in silence for a moment, each wrapped in his own thoughts.

Finally, Kate said, "Max, I want to thank you for helping me tomorrow."

"It is my pleasure, Kate," he said, squeezing her shoulder.

"Perhaps, but I wanted to tell you how much I appreciate it. It is likely that we will not meet after tomorrow. My father's Irish temper may lead him to pack up and take us home."

"Is that not what you want?" he asked.

"Yes, of course, only I would be sorry if we left without my saying thank you."

"I understand. But don't be so glum, Kate. This time tomorrow night, it will all be over."

"Yes, and you will be free to pursue Miss Beauchamp."

"Indeed I shall," he said with relish. Turning to face her, he lifted her chin and said, "I am certain she and I will deal well together, you know. I would not wed her if I did not believe I could . . . grow fond of her."

Kate's eyes shone like black diamonds in the shadow of the moonlight, and she nodded. "I know."

Then she lay her head on his shoulder, and the silence of the night engulfed them.

"Where have you been?" hissed Max the next morning when Kate rode up on Thunderlight.

"I got here as quickly as I could. Is that Palmer's horse?"

"That's the one," said Max, winking at her as he reached up to swing her off the stallion's back. "What did I tell you?"

She managed to keep from laughing. Palmer's horse was close to seventeen hands, every bit as big as Thunderlight. He had a barrel of a body and long, spindly legs — much too spindly to hold all that weight.

Still, when a small groom swung up on the horse's back, Kate almost gasped. Max, now mounted, had no trouble reading her mind.

Leaning down, he said quietly, "Don't worry. The groom may be light, but he's as heavy-handed as his master. Thunderlight and I will have no trouble."

"Nevertheless, I wish you luck, Max," she said, smiling up at him, the energy of the morning race making her heart beat faster. Or was it the handsome man smiling down at her?

Straightening, Max said, "You ready, Palmer?"

"I have been ready," came the imperious reply. "We are agreed as to the course?"

"Agreed. And the stakes?" asked Max.

"Agreed. I will signal the start," said Palmer.

Max hesitated, then nodded, and Palmer took out his handkerchief, lifting it high in the air while Max and the groom jockeyed their horses into position.

Without a word, the handkerchief fluttered to the ground and Palmer's groom drove the big gelding forward with a slap of the whip and a shout. Caught off guard, Max urged Thunderlight to follow.

Kate watched, her heart in her throat. Palmer turned and smiled at her, and she glared in return. The cad! He had done that on purpose!

Soon the two horses and their riders were out of sight, and they waited impatiently for the horses' return.

"What do you reckon, miss? Will he do it?" asked Bobby.

"Of course he will," she snapped at her groom. Immediately, she said, "Forgive me, Bobby. It is just . . ."

"I know, miss. Me, too."

"Care to expand our wager, Miss O'Connor?" called Palmer as the horses came into view again, the gelding leading Thunderlight by a length.

Kate ignored him and yelled, "Come on, Thunderlight! Come on, Max!"

Max was bent over the big horse's neck, urging him ever faster. Kate shouted with laughter when the black stallion leaped forward, closing the gap in two strides and then steadily inching ahead. Seconds later, they whizzed by with Thunderlight decisively in the lead. Bobby and Kate cheered while Palmer cursed.

Max and Thunderlight returned to her side. Slipping to the ground, Max gave her a hug and handed the reins to the groom.

Turning to Palmer, he said, "Bad luck, Palmer."

"Yes, quite," said the other man, who now had himself well in hand. Kate breathed a sigh of relief that things would not get ugly.

"You brought the bill of sale for him?" asked Max.

"No, I did not. Didn't think I would need the da . . . the thing," he amended when Max cocked his head toward Kate. "Sorry. I will have to fetch it from my house."

Max raised a brow, then nodded. "A bit irregular."

"Are you saying I am trying to get out of it?" asked the indignant Palmer.

"No, I merely commented that it is irregular. It is usually better to settle a debt of honor immediately. But I understand perfectly if you forgot," said Max, meeting Palmer's gaze with steely calm.

Palmer looked away first. "Yes, well, it is good of you to understand. Shall we meet here at noon?"

"So late?" said Max. "Make it eleven o'clock, shall we?"

"Very well," said Palmer, sweat breaking out on his brow. "Come along, you fool," he said to his groom. Then he swung up on his gelding, and they rode away.

"Where is he going?" demanded Kate.

"He forgot the bill of sale. I will meet him here at eleven o'clock."

"But, Max, my father is sending Early Girl to Tattersall's this afternoon. Eleven o'clock may well be too late," she said.

"We will have time. Don't worry." When she pursed her lips and raised one brow, he added, "Have I let you down up to now?"

"No."

"Then remember that and quit frowning so. We will have plenty of time. Now, why don't I escort you home while Bobby takes Thunderlight back to the mews for a good rubdown?"

"Very well, but I want to be here when you meet with Palmer," she said.

"I don't think that would be wise, Kate. Men's business, don't you know."

"Nonsense. Thunderlight is my horse, and for that matter, so is Palmer's winded gelding. Do not tell me I should not come," she said, glaring at him with her hands on her hips.

"Very well, but he will not swallow it as easily with a female looking on," said Max.

Her nose in the air, Kate said, "And why should I care to make it easier for Palmer to take? If he has trouble honoring his debt, then he should not wager."

Max chuckled and hooked his arm through hers, pulling her toward the park gate. "You, Miss O'Connor, are a hard woman. You are right, of course," he added, when she flashed angry green eyes his way.

Kate smiled, suddenly in charity with him. "Do you think Gunter's tearoom would be open this early? I have a mind to celebrate."

"Nine o'clock? I doubt it. I know a place where there is always a kettle on. You simply have to slip in through the back entrance. No one will be any the wiser."

"I shouldn't," said Kate, gazing into those deep blue eyes. Then he smiled at her, and she nodded, saying, "Surely there can be no harm in two friends sharing a pot of tea."

"No harm at all," said Max, linking arms with her again. "Our Mrs. Owens makes a creditable tea cake, too."

"It could not be as good as mine," she said.

"You cook, too?" he asked. "How can it be that no man has yet snapped you up, Kate?"

"I suppose most men do not fully appreciate a girl who rides better than they do," she replied, an impish grin on her face.

"Perhaps, but with your grace and beauty, your culinary talents, and your exquisite sense of humor, a man would have to be all about in his head."

"You are quite right, of course," she quipped.

"And modest? Why, such a modest soul," he replied. "Are you certain you do not wish to wed here in London? I am certain if I pointed out these sterling qualities to some of my friends, they would leap at the . . . no? Ah well, it will be England's loss when you return to Ireland."

Kate was laughing by now at his absurdity. How could she not? Their sense of humor was so closely aligned.

"I'll tell you what, my dear girl. I will have Tristram offer for you. He will not feel in the least intimidated by your riding prowess, since he does not ride — unless forced to do so. He would be the perfect mate for you, really. Any time you went out in your carriage, he would be only too happy to allow you to drive."

"An admirable suggestion, my friend, but I am afraid there are two flaws with your plan," said Kate.

"Two flaws? Impossible!"

"Yes, I'm afraid so. First of all, your brother has not shown the least interest in me."

"Oh, well, if you are going to quibble," said Max, his eyes lighting with appreciation.

"And secondly, is he not supposed to wed an heiress also? For truth to tell, I am about as far from being an heiress as . . . as the two of you are!"

Max unlatched the gate leading into his garden from the alleyway and stepped aside to allow Kate to enter first. He then guided her toward the house, along the wall that separated their two properties, to keep anyone from spying her as they entered through the kitchen door.

When they were safe inside, Max continued, "Yes, you are right, but I am loath to let such a prize as you slip through our fingers. Perhaps we could adopt you?"

"Oh, now you are being too absurd," she laughed.

"No, no. Only think. We could remain the best of friends. We could ride together anytime we wished. I am not in the least intimidated by your horsemanship, you must know."

Unable to resist, Kate asked, "And why is that?"

"Quite simple," he said, sitting down beside her on the sofa. "I am a better rider than you are."

"You are not!" she exclaimed, cuffing him on the arm.

"I most certainly am. Do you think you could have ridden Thunderlight to victory today?"

"I most certainly could have. Why, you were only toying with that other horse."

Max laughed, "You are right about that. Well, I didn't wish to make Palmer feel too bad about it. I mean, he tried to do the right thing, letting his groom ride in his stead. But the horse was impossible!"

"And so are you!" she exclaimed.

"Me? What did you want me to do? Lose the race?"

"Of course not," she said.

"Then why would you say such a . . ."

"If you two children cannot play nicely, I will have to separate you," said Tristram, entering the drawing room wearing pantaloons covered by a silk banyan, his feet shoved into his slippers.

"Oh, dear. Did we wake you, Tristram?" asked Kate.

"A good thing if we did," said Max. "He should not be sleeping so late anyway."

"I don't see why he should not sleep late if he wishes," said Kate.

"Well, that is true. It is not as if he is going to go out and accomplish anything."

"Max! How can you say such a thing about Tristram?"

"Indeed," said Tristram, adopting an injured air.

"No, really. Only think about all he has

accomplished. Why, not everyone can say that they have written a book."

"Ah, yes, I forgot about your one flaw," said Max.

"My flaw?" said Kate.

"Yes, you read too much!"

"I do not!"

"Children," said Tristram, holding his head. "If you are going to shout at each other, I am going to leave."

"Then leave," said Max.

"No, we are sorry," said Kate. "No more arguing and teasing, we promise. Don't we, Max?"

Max gave her a big smile and said, "Not right now, anyway. Ah, here is the tea tray. Shall I pour? Or would you care to, Kate?"

"I will pour out," she said.

"Oh, good. Although you know that I can do as good a job at that as you."

"Oh, really," moaned Tristram.

"No, no. That was all. No more, I promise," said Max, accepting a cup from Kate.

Tristram accepted a cup and looked from one to the other before asking, "Well, are you not going to tell me who won the race?"

Max and Kate shared an intimate look, and she nodded, giving Max permission to relate the tale. When he was finished, Tristram expelled a long whistle.

"It sounds like a near-run thing."

"Not at all. Max was magnificent. And so was Thunderlight. They could have taken Palmer's gelding at any time. If he were not such an unpleasant man, I might have felt sorry for him," said Kate.

"Do you think the gelding will bring as much as your mare?" asked Tristram.

"I think so, perhaps more," said Max. "The true horsemen will not bid, but he's a showy thing, and his bloodline is good, so he should fetch a fair price. Speaking of which, we really should be going to get that bill of sale, Kate. It is half past ten."

"No, you go, Max. I have changed my mind. You can meet Palmer alone. I will stay here, if that is all right with Tristram," she said, falling easily into the habit of addressing him by his Christian name, too.

"Not at all. Happy to have the company," said Tristram.

"Your family will not wonder?" asked Max.

"No, I left word with the maid that I was spending the day with a friend, so no one will miss me at home. Just go ahead and then hurry back. We will then confront my father together so he will know he need not sell Early Girl."

"Very well," said Max, taking Kate's hand and kissing it briefly before rising and leaving the room.

When he was gone, Kate put down her cup and sighed. "I hate waiting. I am ever so impatient."

"You and Max. If ever there were two people . . . I am sorry," said Tristram. "I should not have said that."

"Think nothing of it. Your brother and I are alike in many things. I suppose that is what has made us friends. We share so many interests."

"So you do not mind that Max is planning to ask for Philippa Beauchamp's hand?" asked Tristram.

"He is only doing what he has to do, Tristram. It would be unfair of me to get angry over that."

"But if Max did not need to wed an heiress?"

"I have always been a very practical person, Tristram, and since we cannot change our circumstance, I would prefer not to answer that question," she said.

They fell into an awkward silence. Finally, Tristram cleared his throat and said, "Do you play piquet, Kate?"

"Yes, though it is not my best game," she replied politely.

He smiled, reminding her of his dark-haired brother. Picking up a deck of cards, he said, "No matter. We will play for imaginary stakes, so it will not matter that we are both only adequate players."

They played for an hour. Kate was glad of the diversion, for as the time wore on, she wanted to tear at her hair. Waiting had never been a pleasant pastime for her.

Finally, they heard the front door open. The cards were forgotten as they waited for Max to appear. Kate gasped at his grim visage.

"What happened?"

Shaking his head, Max said, "Palmer decided he did not want to lose his precious horse. And that, as you know, was part of the agreement, that whoever lost would have the option of paying cash instead of giving up his horse."

"Did he not pay you?"

Max reached into his pocket and pulled out a purse. He handed it to Kate, who tore it open, spilling the contents onto the table.

"Five hundred pounds? For a racehorse? How could that be a fair price? He would bring twice that at auction."

"Yes, but since Palmer had in his possession his receipt for the horse, which he purchased only this past summer, there was not really anything I could say to dispute his reckoning. His receipt showed that he purchased the gelding for four hundred pounds. After I flattered him about how much more valuable the gelding was after being properly trained by him, he agreed to up the price to five hundred guineas. It is still not a great sum. I am sorry, Kate."

"Oh, Max," she said. "What am I to do now? That will never be enough. Papa will still feel he has to sell Early Girl."

"I have an idea," said Tristram.

They both swung around to stare.

"Max, why not go to Tattersall's and buy the mare? Perhaps five hundred will be sufficient."

"That is an idea," said Max.

"Furthermore, I have another fifty guineas you may have," said Tristram.

"Oh, no, Tristram. I could not allow you to do that," said Kate.

"But I want to. Here, Max, add this to the purse," said Tristram, placing his own coins on the table with the others.

"I think we must let him do it, Kate. When a fellow has a mind to be noble, we

196

should not stand in his way," said Max.

"Very well," she said, rising and kissing Tristram on the cheek. Turning back to Max, she said firmly, "I'm coming with you."

"No!" said both brothers at once.

"Out of the question!" said Max.

"That is not a good idea, Kate," added Tristram.

"I really do not care what you say, either of you. Early Girl is my horse, and I am going to Tattersall's either to buy her or to say good-bye."

She glared at each of them in turn. Tristram merely shrugged his shoulders. Max opened his mouth to protest, but when Kate put her hands on her hips, he threw up his hands in surrender.

"Very well, but you cannot go dressed like that. You would never get inside. Tristram, what do we have that might fit Master O'Connor?"

As Kate and Max entered the huge stables that resembled a Greek temple, she whispered reverently, "Tattersall's. I never thought I would get to see the inside of it."

"Sh! If you want to stay, keep quiet. I have no desire to have you thrown out. Your father would have me horsewhipped, and rightly so, for bringing you along," said Max.

"Sh!" she replied, pulling her hat farther down on her face.

Kate was not really concerned about people guessing her identity. With her height, no one would guess she was not a young man. She wore one of Tristram's coats over his shirt, the collars arranged so high that the nape of her neck and that flame red hair were covered. In lieu of the usual cravat, Barton had found a hideous spotted neckerchief that fell over the front of her coat, hiding her generous curves.

She looked up to find Max grinning at her. Her eyes flashing, Kate hissed, "What are you laughing at?"

"Nothing, Master O'Connor," he replied. "I want you to wait here while I go find out when the mare will be brought out."

Kate nodded and watched him saunter closer to the ring. At the moment, a large gray hunter was on the block. The bidding was quite high, so Kate guessed that the horse, or his owner, had a reputation.

Suddenly her breath caught in her throat. Palmer and his friend Osgood walked through the doors to her right. She tried to melt into the woodwork as they passed in front of her. When they paused, Kate attempted to sidle away.

Turning, Osgood said, "Oh, sorry, young man. We didn't see you there. Didn't mean to stand in your way. Come on up and stand in front of us."

Seeing no way to avoid complying without speaking, Kate mumbled a gruff thank you and moved forward. The hair on the back of her neck stood on end when she saw Max returning. Her eyes signaled him to look behind her, and she breathed a sigh of relief when he passed her by. Extending a hand to greet both Palmer and Osgood, Max put himself between her and them.

"Surprised to see you here, Darby," said Palmer.

"I was about to say the same," drawled Max. "It is not as if you needed to replace a horse."

Palmer stiffened, and Osgood laughed, saying, "Good one, Darby. Palmer is forever going on about that horse of his. I guess he was not as fast as you thought, eh, Palmer?"

"No, and that is why I have decided to sell him after all. He's coming up next."

Max jumped as Kate put her foot down on his heel.

"Really? Then if he sells for more than the five hundred, you will not mind paying me the rest of my winnings."

Palmer snarled, "We already settled, Darby."

"We settled on what you said was a fair price, but if, three hours later, you sell the animal for, say, a thousand, I will expect to be paid the difference."

"It makes perfect sense to me," said Osgood, as his friend turned an ugly shade of purple.

"And I'm telling you it is no better than robbery," said Palmer, his voice rising so that other men close by were beginning to notice.

Kate scurried back to the shadows as Max continued, "How can a horse be worth one value at eleven o'clock and another at two o'clock? If you were to pay for losing that race with either your horse or his value, then honor dictates that you do so."

"Do you question my honor?" demanded Palmer.

Max stood chest to chest with the man and looked him in the eye. "That depends. Will you pay me fairly? I understand your hoping to unload the beast before people find out he lost the match race against Thunderlight."

"It is nothing of the sort!" exclaimed Palmer.

"You cannot have it both ways, Palmer," said his friend Osgood.

"Very well, I will pull him from the sale!" said Palmer.

"Suit yourself," replied Max.

Palmer took a step in the direction of the platform, then paused as he took in all the accusing stares around him.

Turning back, he glared at Max and said, "Devil take you, Darby. Have it your way. Whatever Pinnacle sells for, I will pay you anything over five hundred."

"Why, thank you, Palmer," said Max, his expression nonchalant.

As the bidding began, he sidled close to Kate, winking at her. She bit her lip to keep from laughing. Then her attention was caught by the big bay gelding being led into the ring. Her smile widened as the bidding topped five hundred, ending with a final bid of nine hundred and fifty pounds.

"Gilroy Beck," muttered Max as the new owner went forward. "Another wily horseman."

"Sh!" hissed Kate.

A few minutes later, Palmer stalked up

to Max and thrust the four hundred and fifty guineas into his hand.

"There!" he said. His glare fell on Max and then on Kate. His eyes narrowed, and his lips twisted into a snarl. Tipping his hat, he stalked away, but not before saying, "Good day, Miss O'Connor."

Then he was gone, and Kate had to hold onto Max to keep herself steady as her knees buckled.

"Max, he recognized me," she whispered.

"Don't worry. He will not dare to expose us. We know too much about him." Kate frowned a question, and he added, "When I went to meet with him for the bill of sale, I mentioned that I thought his manner of starting the race was a bit havey-cavey. However, since the outcome was in our favor, I was not going to press the matter."

"What did he say?"

Max shrugged. "Can't repeat that to a lady."

"Oh," murmured Kate as this information sank in. Then she asked, "How much longer?"

"Two, perhaps three more before Early Girl. I know you love her, but I do not think the bidding will go much past eight hundred."

"Perhaps we should just go and tell Papa," she said.

"In this place?" asked Max, casting a glance around the smoky male audience. "How is his temper? Would he take the news that his daughter had gone against his express wishes and come to Tattersall's calmly?"

"Never mind," she said, pulling her hat even lower over her face.

"The next horse is Early Girl, a proven broodmare out of . . ." began the announcer in the ring.

"I cannot bear to watch," said Kate, starting for the door. She had thought it would be interesting, but the suspense was unbearable. Max, however, was not ready to let her go, for he took her by the elbow and kept her by his side.

"You cannot leave now. How would you get home?"

Kate's green eyes, practically the only part of her face showing, begged him to understand.

Max smiled and said calmly, "Don't worry, Kate. I can handle this. In a few minutes, Early Girl will be all yours."

Gazing into those deep blue eyes, Kate felt a peace come over her. Though she might be naive, she felt a perfect confidence in Max at that moment. With a nod, she turned back to watch as he placed his first bid.

"I have two hundred from the gentleman in the back," said the announcer. "And three hundred from the gentleman on my left. Do I hear four?"

Max nodded, and the announcer continued. Kate began to fidget as the price rose — six, seven, eight hundred. Kate searched frantically for the person bidding against Max, but she could not guess who it might be.

Max nodded again, and the announcer said, "Eight hundred fifty. Do I hear nine hundred? Nine hundred to you, sir."

"All done? I am selling the mare for eight hundred and fifty guineas to Mr. Darby."

Kate threw her arms around his neck, and Max laughed, quickly removing her arms. To the interested onlookers, he said, "A gift for my young cousin from the country."

Kate quickly stepped back into the shadows while Max went forward to pay for the mare and lead her out of the ring. When they were safely away from Tattersall's, Kate linked arms with him, grinning hugely.

"Thank you, Max! If we were not in public, I would throw my arms around your neck again and kiss you!"

He shot her a wicked look and began leading the mare more quickly. Kate had to step lively to keep up with his pace.

Soon, she demanded, "Why are we rushing so?"

"I am looking for the closest place that is *not* public," he replied, giving her another wicked smile.

"Wretch!" she said with a gurgle of laughter.

Seven

"Papa is going to be furious at first, Max. I really think you should let me speak to him alone." Kate, who had changed back to her riding habit by now, was matching Max stride for stride as they headed for her house.

"I will do nothing of the sort. I refuse to play the coward. I know very well that you will not bother to tell him that the entire plan was my idea," said Max, planting one foot stubbornly in the opening of her front door.

Kate had no choice but to step aside and allow him to enter. They had already spent thirty minutes at the stables, delivering Early Girl and giving MacAfee an abbreviated explanation. Kate was quite certain the head groom had wanted to punch Max in the nose, and only her presence had stopped him.

Her father's reaction would be even worse, and she had sworn Mr. MacAfee to silence. She had even persuaded him to keep Early Girl hidden until she had had a chance to speak to her father. Her father had a quick temper, and anyone nearby was considered fair game.

"Come this way," said Kate, leading him to the small drawing room. "Thank heavens Mama is visiting my aunt today. By the time she gets home, Papa's temper should have cooled. Perhaps he will not even want to mention this to her."

"Kate, surely your father will be too pleased with the results to question our methods too closely."

"Oh, he will eventually be laughing about it, calling me his clever puss, but that may take a month . . . or twelve."

Max chuckled and said, "At least he is an honest man, not an inveterate gambler like my father. When we were children, my twin and I, our family owned a great deal of land. We had horses and carriages. After my mother died, I suppose it was, my father started gambling. He would be gone for a month or two, then come home and tell us this parcel of land, or that parcel, had been sold. It wasn't until we were older that we understood what was happening."

"How terrible for you, losing your mother and your father like that," said Kate.

Max cocked his head to one side. "I had

never thought of it like that, but you are right. I suppose, in a very real way, we did. That is why Tristram has so little patience for our father. He has never been close to him. Monty and I, on the other hand, remember how he used to be, always happy and singing. He used to sing to our mother all the time."

"That is so sad, Max," said Kate, reaching out and touching his arm. He covered her hand, causing her to shiver, shocked by the warmth his touch had set off inside her.

"Mary Katherine O'Connor!"

They leaped apart guiltily. Max rose and went to stand by the fireplace. Kate smoothed her habit and tried to fight down the overwhelming sense of panic that had taken hold of her.

"In here, Papa," she called before saying to Max, "I guess he spotted Early Girl."

Kieran O'Connor threw open the drawing room door and demanded, "Mary Katherine O'Connor! What is the meaning of that mare of yours being back in my stable?"

Max stepped forward, and Mr. O'Connor glared at him. Kate waved him away. With a grimace, Max retreated to the fireplace.

"Papa, why do you not sit down while I explain?"

"I will sit down after the explanation, young lady. And what is he doing here?"

"I have had a part in this, sir, and I did not wish to leave your daughter to face you alone," said Max.

"Leave my daughter to face me alone? Why, you young whelp, I'll teach you to . . ."

Kate jumped between them, her hands on her father's heaving chest. "Papa, stop it this instant! You will not fight Mr. Darby, not when he has been such a good friend to me, to all of us."

Her father transferred his furious glare to her, and she shrank away from him. This action seemed to have an effect on him, and he stepped back, too.

With a final grunt of anger, he sat down on the sofa, crossed him arms, and said, "Out with it, my girl!"

Kate then related how Max had come to her rescue when she was so upset that her father was selling Early Girl.

Beyond another grunt, her father's only response was, "I told you, Mary Kate. It was business."

"Yes, Papa, but it was making me miserable, and Max wanted to help."

"Max?" said her father, eyeing the young man suspiciously.

"Mr. Max Darby. There are two of them next door, Papa. It gets very confusing to always be calling them Mr. Darby and having them wonder which one you are talking to."

"Very well. Get along with your story."

"Anyway, Max thought it might be profitable to . . . um, well, that is . . . ."

Max stepped forward, touching Kate's shoulder until her father's glare made him drop his hand. Still, he said, "I convinced Kate that she should let me arrange another match race for Thunderlight."

Mr. O'Connor leaped to his feet and shouted, "You raced my horse without my permission, young lady?"

"She didn't ride him, sir. I did," said Max.

Kate's father was stunned, and he sat down again. "When? Where? And more importantly, against whom?"

"Early this morning, in the park, against Palmer's gelding, Pinnacle."

Forgetting his anger, Mr. O'Connor, the horseman, said, "By Jove! And you took him by how many lengths?"

Max pulled up the chair next to Mr. O'Connor and said, "It was a beautiful race, sir. I could have taken him sooner, but I let him have the lead. His groom was playing jockey, and he is a fairly good rider, but I knew we could overtake him."

"Tell him about the start, Max," urged Kate.

"Oh, yes, the start. Well, this is for your ears only, but Palmer started the race himself, dropping his handkerchief without so much as a 'ready, steady.' "

"Really? And you didn't call him on it?"

"I told him I would remember," said Max, and Kate's father nodded approvingly. "But back to the race. The gelding leaped ahead. It was quite obvious that they had arranged the start beforehand. I urged Thunderlight on, but I didn't try to overtake him until the last leg, when we were returning to the starting point. Then he gave me his all. It was beautiful," said Max.

"Absolutely beautiful," echoed Kate, causing her father to remember her presence and her part in the deception, for he gave her a fierce frown.

Turning back to Max, O'Connor smiled and said, "But you won."

"That we did, sir."

"And then you brought the gelding to the sale ring at Tattersall's and with the

211

proceeds, you bid on my daughter's mare, buying her back for Kate."

"Something like that, sir," said Max, sharing a smile with Kate. No need for them to tell her father that Kate had gone to Tattersall's, too.

"I see. So the money in my pocket is really the winnings from the match race with Palmer's gelding, which you won on the back of my horse, Thunderlight."

"Yes, sir, except for the other one hundred guineas which Kate has in her reticule there."

"Oh, yes, Papa. I almost forgot." She handed him the remainder of the winnings with a smile.

He stared at the coins in his hand for a moment. Finally, he looked up with a smile and said, "You, my daughter, are a minx. A cunning one, to be sure, but a minx."

"Yes, Papa," she replied with an impish grin.

"Very well, the two of you seem to have gotten away with this shocking scheme this time, but no more such shenanigans, do you hear, Mary Kate?"

They agreed and breathed a sigh of relief, but it was premature.

"Now, Kate, why don't you go and see if you can talk Cook out of some refreshments for all of us. I want to speak to Mr. Darby alone for a few minutes."

Kate rose and frowned down at her father. "You will not fight him, will you, Papa? Nor will you lecture him."

"Run along with you, girl."

When Kate was gone, the two men stared at each other for a moment before the older man spoke.

"Mr. Darby, you are a man of the world, are you not?"

"I suppose so," said Max.

"My daughter, for all her straightforward manners, is not very worldly. She is an innocent. What's more, she is mine, and I do not wish to see her hurt — by anyone."

"I would not dream of hurting Kate."

"And yet you sat here earlier this week and said you plan to wed another girl, did you not?"

Max shifted uncomfortably in his chair. "Yes, sir, I did. I still do. I really have little choice in the matter."

"Well, I appreciate your candor, and I understand a man wanting and needing to better himself."

"I really believe, sir, that Kate understands all this. I do not think she is in danger of forming a *tendre* for me. I have made no secret about my plans to wed Miss Beauchamp."

"That's good to know, but a father worries about his only child, his only daughter."

"You need not worry on my account, Mr. O'Connor."

"Good. So have you come up with a plausible explanation why you bought a mare at Tattersall's and it has ended up in my daughter's possession again? What is Society going to think? You can hardly tell them the truth."

"I . . . I had not considered that," said Max. In truth, he had not thought beyond making Kate smile again. That had been his goal, and when he had achieved it, he, too, had been happy.

"You should have, my boy, but do not worry too much. I have a solution."

"To what, Papa?" asked Kate, returning to the drawing room.

"How we can explain your having Early Girl again."

"Explain to whom?" asked Kate.

Her father once again voiced his concern. Then he said, "I propose that you, Mr. Darby, will begin to ride Thunderlight. We will tell everyone that we have worked out a trade, that my daughter's unhappiness over losing her pet mare made me reconsider. No one will question your wanting to swap the mare for the stallion."

"And when you return to Ireland and take the stallion with you?" asked Max.

"By then the possibility of scandal attaching itself to my girl's good name will have passed. She, hopefully, will be settled with a husband, and you will be wed, too," said Mr. O'Connor.

Watching Kate, Max nodded. She made a little face, but she did not disagree with her father's plan. On his part, it was an excellent solution, and the idea of riding Thunderlight any time he wished was superb.

Just then, Mrs. O'Connor returned, sweeping into the room and kissing her husband's cheek. She smiled at Max and urged Kate to follow her upstairs to see all the ribbons and trims she had purchased.

"But we were waiting for the tea tray, Mama," said Kate.

"I really should be going, Kate. Good day, Mrs. O'Connor, Mr. O'Connor."

"Must you go so soon, Mr. Darby?" said Kate's mother.

"Yes, I have an engagement this evening. Good day."

Forgetting about their guest and turning to Kate, her mother said, "Goodness, yes,

Kate. You should be resting before the Laceys' ball tonight." She smiled at Max and said, "Good day, Mr. Darby. Do call again."

Kate walked with him to the door where he bowed over her hand. "Are you going to the Laceys' ball tonight?"

"I would not miss it," he replied.

Kate answered this comment with a smile and a wink.

He nodded and was gone.

"Master Max, there is a note arrived from the marquess," said Barton, when Max returned from the O'Connor house.

"What now?" grumbled Max, tearing open the envelope. "Wonderful. We are to pick up both the marquess and my father on our way to the Laceys' ball tonight. Tristram will be ecstatic," he added dryly.

"Ecstatic about what?" asked his brother, who had just arrived home. Max related the contents of the note, and Tristram gave an unaccustomed laugh.

"What is so funny? I thought you would be, at the very least, annoyed."

"What is the point? Besides, we are all going to the same place. We might as well go together." The clock over the fireplace began to chime, and he added sunnily,

"Time to get dressed."

When he was gone, Max and the servant shared a puzzled frown. Shaking his head, Max headed for his own room.

"Would you bring me something to eat, Barton? I will starve if I have to wait until the midnight supper they usually have at these things."

"Certainly, sir," said the servant, hurrying away.

An hour later, the four men were seated in the marquess's spacious carriage, heading to Richmond, where the Laceys had a palatial mansion along the river, in the Italian style.

"Why don't you and Lady Anne build something like this for your honeymoon home?" said the marquess.

"Shaddup," grumbled the viscount, glaring at each of the others in turn.

"What is this, Papa? Have you been holding out on us?" teased Tristram.

"No, I ain't holding out on you. I'm holding out on Lady Anne, and a very tricky affair it is."

The marquess gave a cackle and informed the brothers, "Lady Anne has told him in no uncertain terms that she means to have him. He, however, is being stubborn. Why, I don't know. She's as rich as

Croesus and almost as powerful, in her way."

"Why?" asked the viscount. "Have you looked at her lately? I mean, really looked at her? She looks like a bulldog with those great jowls of hers. And that figure — if one can call it that!"

His sons laughed at this, earning themselves another glare.

"Why has she settled on you, Papa?" asked Max.

"Oh, she has had a *tendre* for me since her come-out some forty years ago. I had enough trouble shaking loose from her then, but she finally had to accept it when I married your mother," he said. "But this time . . ."

"This time, you should simply close your eyes and leap at the old witch's offer," said the marquess with a gleeful cackle. "She would have no trouble settling all your debts."

"Yes, but she doesn't like gambling or drinking or smoking, and I like all of those things. She would try to reform me," he added in horrified tones.

"Perhaps you could bring her around, Papa," said Tristram, hardly containing his laughter.

"And perhaps pigs can fly," snapped his

father. "I don't want to talk about it. We are here, and she will probably be here waiting. I have to keep my wits about me," he said, throwing open the door and climbing down the steps before the carriage rolled to a stop.

By the time the other three occupants of the carriage had descended, the viscount had already disappeared.

"She'll catch him," said the marquess with another wheezing cackle. Looking at them each in turn, he added with a sneer, "You two boys see that you catch your own mates." With this advice, the bony marquess left them.

"What do you make of all that?" said Max.

"I would like to think that it means Papa is going to have the opportunity to repair the family fortunes on his own. However, given his history of irresponsibility, I take leave to doubt it will ever happen," said Tristram.

"I don't know. Lady Anne seems quite determined."

The two brothers strolled into the house, which boasted black and white marble tiles throughout the ground floor. Green palms waved at them from behind pillars and groupings of delicate French chairs dotted the large, open foyer. They followed other guests up the stairs to the first floor and greeted their host and hostess.

Mr. James Lacey had earned his money through savvy business dealings, but being the younger son of an earl, he was still accepted by a society that looked down on earned money. His wife, a flighty woman whose father was a country squire, was known for her lavish entertaining. In warmer Seasons, they gave sumptuous alfresco breakfasts. This evening, the ball would be indoors — a sad crush, despite the fact that several drawing rooms and a ballroom opened onto each other.

The first people to spy the Darby brothers were the O'Connors. Dragging her mother after her, Kate smiled and curtsied to them.

Turning back to her mother, she said, "Mama, may I present Mr. Tristram Darby. I don't believe you two have met."

The introductions quickly dispensed with, Kate's mother said, "Is this not a lovely home?"

"Yes, the Laceys are known for their entertainments," replied Tristram. "And listen to that music. The very best musicians, to be sure. A waltz, I think. Would you care to dance, Mrs. O'Connor?"

"Oh, I am not very good at the waltz, young man," said the matron with a blush.

"Nonsense, Mama. You and papa have often waltzed. Go on. You will enjoy yourself."

"But you, my dear . . ."

Max took his cue and said, "If she will have me, I would be honored to dance with your daughter."

"Thank you, Max," said Kate, smiling up at him and taking his hand.

Max gave a nod to his brother, acknowledging his adroitness in maneuvering Kate into his company. Then Max glanced down at Kate, who wore a cream-colored gown with emerald green trim. He tore his gaze away from the creamy rise of her full breasts and smiled into her eyes.

"You are beautiful, Kate," he said without thinking. "The green on your gown matches your eyes perfectly."

She turned pink with pleasure and whispered, "How kind of you to notice, after all the hours I searched for this trim."

"Your efforts were not wasted, my dear," he said softly as he guided her around the dance floor, his hand on her back and the other holding her hand.

Out of the corner of his eye, he saw the arrival of the Beauchamp family. Mrs.

Beauchamp waved as they sailed past.

Clearing his throat, Max continued more sensibly, "Has your father gotten over his anger?"

"Oh yes. It never lasts for long. I am back to being simply 'Kate' again," she said with a chuckle. His eyes narrowed, and she explained, "When Papa is really angry, I am 'Mary Katherine O'Connor.' When he is less angry, 'Mary Katherine.' Then 'Mary Kate' and finally, when he is back to his usual self, I am once again 'Kate.'"

"Then I am glad you are merely 'Kate' again. And how is Early Girl after her near miss?"

"I sent to the stables to find out, and MacAfee said she is quite happy to be back in her own stall. Max, I cannot thank you enough."

He gave her hand a squeeze and grinned down at her, his gaze admiring. Kate returned that smile. Their rotation around the room had lead them back to the spot where the Beauchamps were standing and watching.

Glancing their way, Max's smile faded, and he commented politely, "Fine weather we are having. I do hope it holds."

Kate's own smile froze and faded away.

As they continued their circuit of the room, Max grew more frustrated. The girl in his arms was perfect in every way — except for fortune. She was closer to his height and fit perfectly in his arms. He imagined waltzing with Miss Beauchamp, and his lip curled with disdain. She would certainly not be gazing up at him admiringly. He would probably not even be able to see her face. It would be permanently fixed on his waistcoat.

"Is something wrong, Max? You suddenly look angry or upset about something," said Kate, concern in her eyes.

He shook his head, tightened his hold, and twirled her recklessly through the other dancers. Onto the balcony they waltzed, where other couples, also in search of a stolen moment of privacy, lingered.

Dancing her toward the far corner, Max stopped suddenly. His hands slid to her bare arms, and he studied her fiercely for a moment before pulling her close. Kate melted against him, molding her body to his as their lips met in a fiery kiss.

Then it was over. He set her at arm's length and shook his head.

Agony in his face and voice, he said, "I cannot, Kate. I . . ."

"Cannot what?" she asked.

"You know. I cannot go on like this. Every time we meet, it becomes clearer and clearer to me that . . . but I cannot do this. I must not. I have to . . . Miss Beauchamp . . . I . . ."

Kate stepped away so that his hands dropped to his sides. "I understand, Max. I am sorry. I wish . . . but it was not meant to be, and I do understand. You have a responsibility to your family — to your father and your brothers." She stepped around him. Placing a hand on his arm, she added, "I wish you much happiness. Always."

He touched her hand until she slipped away, returning to the ballroom. Max peered into the darkness, gathering his wits and his courage. Redoubling his resolution, he returned to the ballroom in search of the wealthy Miss Beauchamp.

He had no difficulty spotting her, along with her mother. This time, however, her mother appeared bent on playing the part of chaperon. She was keeping Palmer at arm's length from Philippa, but as soon as Max appeared, she practically handed Philippa to him.

"There is our Mr. Darby," she gushed. "You see, I told you so, Mr. Palmer. I told you he had claimed dear Philippa's first dance. A shame it cannot be a waltz like the last one, eh, Mr. Darby?"

"There is something to be said for the quadrille," said Max dully.

Philippa's blue eyes sought his for a moment, and her brow puckered adorably. Then she took the hand he offered and followed him onto the floor for the next dance.

"I trust you are well this evening," he said formally.

"Yes, thank you."

They made it through that set by dint of civilities. When it was over, Max returned her to her mother. Philippa was claimed for the next dance, and Max slunk away, loitering on the edge of the dance floor, as far from Mrs. Beauchamp as he could get.

Watching Kate with each subsequent partner was exquisite torture, but it was only what he deserved. How could he have been so stupid as to make her fall in love with him? For he had seen the love in her eyes. There had been no denying it. He had hurt her with his . . . betrayal. No matter if she had known he could not, they could not . . .

Hell and blast!

He turned on his heel and went in

search of something strong and lethal. In the card room set up for people who did not wish to dance, Max found full decanters and helped himself to a generous portion of brandy.

"Take it easy on that, my boy," said Mr. Beauchamp. "You will need your wits about you tonight. Or are you already celebrating?"

Max glared at the older man and said, "I don't know what you are talking about, Mr. Beauchamp."

"I thought Philippa might have told you, but there. My girl is so shy, she probably could not bring herself to broach the matter, especially here in public."

"I still do not understand, sir."

"Why, that she has decided to accept you. She is quite fond of you, I believe."

"Your daughter? Fond of me?"

"Yes, indeed. And I have taken the liberty of asking our host, who is a particular friend of mine, if we might make the announcement here tonight. What do you think?"

Max looked from Philippa's father to the full glass in his hand. He lifted the glass and drained it.

"Why not? It will make this evening complete."

"Excellent. Come along. I'll go and find Lacey and meet you near the musicians. We'll have them play a little fanfare to gain everyone's attention. Come along, my boy," said the short man, pulling Max after him.

James Lacey stepped onto the musician's platform as the dance ended. After a quick, whispered consultation, the musicians played a fanfare, capturing the attention of all the guests. Mr. Beauchamp joined Lacey on the platform.

"My lords, ladies, and gentlemen, my good friend Robert Beauchamp has an announcement to make."

A little gasp of excitement rippled through the crowd.

Beauchamp cleared his throat and said, "First of all, I would like my Philippa to join me here on the platform. Come along, my dear child."

The guests parted to allow his pink-cheeked daughter to reach the platform. He took her hand and pulled her close to his side.

With a signal to Max to join them, he continued, "I am pleased to announce the betrothal of my only child to a fine young man, Maxwell Darby." This caused a gasp from the other guests, and then came a round of polite applause.

Max forced a smile to his lips as he gazed across the congested ballroom. In the sea of faces, one stood out, and his smile faded. Kate, white as a sheet. Then she turned away.

Max remained rooted to the floor while the army of footmen passed among the guests, distributing champagne for a toast. Mrs. Beauchamp joined them on the platform, too.

Putting her hand on Max's arm, she whispered huskily, "At least you will always be close by, my dear Max."

Lacey raised his glass and said, "To the happy couple."

Everyone drank to their happiness. Max downed his in a single gulp. He noticed that Philippa did the same.

Then the moment had passed, and the musicians struck up another dance. Max turned to his betrothed and took her hand without asking for permission. He knew what was expected of him now, and he was grimly determined to comply.

As they headed onto the dance floor, he passed his father, who said, "Well done, my boy. Now perhaps I can escape."

Max glared at his father and then laughed, a hollow sound. Spying Lady

Anne's approach behind his parent, he said spitefully, "I wouldn't speak too soon, Papa. Your day is coming, too."

"How delightful for you, my boy," said Lady Anne, kissing his cheek. She smiled at Philippa and said, "Now, do not be jealous, my dear. It is the father that I am interested in. I hope to soon be hearing the same joyous news myself. Now, Tavistoke, you promised to be my partner at whist. Come along, my dear."

Max and Miss Beauchamp made up a set with three other couples, among them Tristram, who was partnering a chattering girl with frizzy brown hair and a large nose. Tristram looked about as miserable as a young man could without breaking the rules of propriety, but he cocked his head and gave a quizzical frown when he saw Max's black mood.

Standing next to his brother and Miss Beauchamp, Tristram commented, "Allow me to offer my congratulations." Max grunted, and Tristram added, "This has turned into quite an exciting event, has it not?"

Max grimaced, but Miss Beauchamp said, "Oh, yes, Mr. Darby. And is this not the perfect setting? Of course, the Laceys' home is also quite impressive in the daylight. Have you ever seen it then, Mr. Darby? And in the spring, the grounds are simply breathtaking."

Max's head swung around in amazement. Miss Beauchamp was actually speaking? And in complete sentences? What magic had his brother worked?

When she spied him looking down at her, Philippa again ducked her head. The music started, and they were forced to pay attention to the movements of the dance.

Max had no difficulty avoiding conversation. His fierce frown kept his betrothed from uttering so much as a squeak. By the time the music ended, Max's mood had sunk to such a level that he could have cheerfully throttled her or put a gun to his own head. And each time he looked at Tristram, his happy-go-lucky brother who was not betrothed, he wanted to include him in the planned mayhem hatching in his brain.

As Max escorted Philippa back to her mother, she shrank against him, and he looked down at her with a quizzical expression.

"What is it, Miss Beauchamp?"

"Nothing."

She appeared to be tugging on his arm, trying to slow their progress. He stopped and turned to her, saying, "It must be something. Do you not wish to return to your mother?"

She shook her head. Max, who could only agree with this sentiment, turned in another direction and felt the girl at his side heave a sigh of relief.

"Are you going to tell me what that was all about?" he asked.

"It was not my mother, but the man beside her. I did not wish to dance with him."

Max frowned until he recalled who had been standing beside Mrs. Beauchamp. "Palmer? What is wrong with Palmer?"

"He . . . I do not like the way he studies me." Biting at her lower lip, she continued, "Like I am a mouse, and he is a cat. It is most disconcerting."

Max smiled down at the girl, his first real smile for her, and she was not immune to its effect, for she returned it, shyly.

It brought out the knight errant in him, and he said, "I'll take care of Palmer. You need not worry about him ever again."

"Oh, thank you, Mr. Darby."

"You are welcome. Now, here comes my brother, and since it is the waltz they are striking up, I think he would be a safe partner for my future bride."

This speech made her drop her gaze, but he was happy to think that she had at least confided in him in this small matter. Perhaps he had not made such a horrendous mistake. Perhaps they could learn to rub along together reasonably well.

"Tristram, I am charging you with looking after my fiancée for the duration of this waltz. Are you willing and able?" he quipped.

"More than willing, Max. Philippa, will you do me the honor?"

"Oh, yes, thank you, Tristram," she said, going happily with him onto the dance floor.

Watching them with a puzzled gaze, Max felt a bony hand on his shoulder. He cringed when he realized it was the Marquess of Cravenwell.

"Well done, my boy. Make certain you do not let Beauchamp bamboozle you with the settlements. It won't do you any good if he ties everything up for any offspring she may produce."

"Must you be constantly harping about money?" asked Max.

"It has always amused me how people without money insist that it is not the most important thing in the world. Those of us who have it know that it is." Cackling at his own witticism, the marquess strolled away.

Max saw Tristram waltz by with Philippa and frowned again. Funny that they addressed each other by their Christian names. He shrugged.

Then he watched as Kate spun by in the arms of Palmer. Her face was fixed with a glassy smile — one that had started out as polite but had faded as it froze there. Then her eyes met his, and he could have sworn he saw tears there.

Max fought the nearly overwhelming urge to race forward and tear her out of Palmer's arms. Each time they passed, the feeling grew, until, finally, he had to turn away.

Blindly, he walked through the onlookers, answering their congratulations with a terse nod. He felt as if his throat were closing, and his chest were about to burst. A ripple of laughter made him pause, thinking he was the target of someone's amusement.

He turned to face the small knot of girls who had no partners and were merely watching the dancers. They were all but schoolgirls, and he started to turn until two words caught his attention — *Miss Tattersall's*. As this was followed by titters of laughter and pointing toward the dancers, his attention was caught. Kate swept by again, her face full of misery.

"Can you imagine why any respectable female would want to go there?" said one miss.

"What can one expect of the daughter of an Irish horse seller?" said another with a giggle.

Max let out a growl of disgust, and the girls scattered.

Across the ballroom now, Kate's eyes again met his. He waited, watching as Palmer guided her around the edge of the floor. Reaching out, he neatly yanked the unsuspecting Palmer away from Kate. With two smooth steps, Max took his place, pulling Kate into his arms and continuing the waltz with hardly a ripple in the movements of the other dancers. Only a few people saw the astonishing swap, but those who did immediately commented on the transformation of Miss O'Connor's face. Her smile could not have been brighter.

And wasn't it odd that Mr. Darby's smile appeared more genuine than it had when his betrothal was announced?

Most odd, said those in the know.

Eight

"Never let it be said that the Darby men have too much sense for their own good," said Tristram, looking from his brother to his father the afternoon following the Laceys' ball. "You, Papa, made a perfect cake of yourself, losing all that money at whist and then allowing Lady Anne to settle the debt for you."

"It was her debt, too. We were partners!" exclaimed his father, holding his head at the effort this speech had caused him. "Devil take you, boy, it is not right to ring a peal over a man after a night of drowning his sorrows."

"Someone has to talk sense to you," said Tristram.

"But I am not half as bad as that brother of yours," said the viscount.

"And may the devil take you, old man," muttered Max. "At least I did not embarrass myself in front of all my friends. You will be lucky if you are allowed to play anywhere after that scene."

"And at least I am not going to get myself killed in some idiotic duel!" yelled his father. "How could you be so stupid, boy? Haven't I taught you better than that?"

"You? Teach me? When did you ever teach me anything except by showing me the road *not* to travel?" yelled Max. "Besides, I am not going to get myself killed. You know perfectly well that Palmer is no match for me with pistols or rapiers."

"So you will only be thrown in prison for killing your man," said the viscount.

"It seems to me," said Tristram, "that is what brought us to London in the first place, trying to keep you out of prison, Papa. Now, let us quit squabbling and see what can be done."

The viscount hunched his shoulders, but he leaned forward to listen. Max, however, folded his arms and remained aloof, glaring at his father and brother in turn.

Finally, he said, "I shan't kill the bastard, though he richly deserves it. Miss Beauchamp says he makes her feel like a mouse, and he is the cat. Palmer's a nasty fellow all the way around, and if you are trying to get me to issue an apology, you can forget it, for I won't."

"Spoken like a five year old," said Tristram. When Max stood up, he said hastily, "No, no, do not run off. We have some repair work to do. First of all, Papa, I want to show you something."

Tristram pulled out his sketchbook and opened it. With a few quick strokes, he had outlined a table with cards strewn upon it and a man and woman sitting across from each other.

"That's very good, son, but I don't see . . ."

"No, you would not. Max, would you care to tell our father about the stir I created last year, selling my little drawings to the scandal sheets?"

"I never knew that," said the viscount. "Selling them, you say?"

Max laughed at the memory and said, "It was quite a stir. He drew a picture of Adele Landis, the heiress Monty was courting. You know, our Clarissa's cousin, the shrew."

"Oh, yes, but what about Tristram's drawing?"

"It depicted a spider, with Adele's face, on her web. Trapped there, too, were Monty and Benchley, struggling to get free," said Max.

"But what about the one where I drew her as Medusa? That made quite a splash, too," said Tristram with a laugh as he continued to draw. When he was satisfied, he held it out to his father. "See, Papa, this will put everything in a new light. You will no longer be seen as a kept man."

"I'll be seen as a kept husband!" protested the viscount, throwing the sketchbook to the floor. "What are you thinking, showing me looking at Lady Anne like a lovesick puppy?"

"Only this: If people think you are truly in love with her, no one will question your marrying her and accepting her money."

"He has a valid point, Papa," said Max, unable to contain his laughter anymore. His brother joined in while their father fumed.

"That's all well and good for the two of you to laugh, but you're not having to marry the blasted bulldog."

"Papa, she is a very nice bulldog, uh, lady, and I think she genuinely cares for you. Why don't you just give in?" said Tristram.

Turning the tables, the viscount said, "What do you have in mind for Max? Everyone thinks he's a madman, announcing his betrothal to one girl and then getting into a duel over another one. There's nothing you can do about that with your blasted drawings."

"Oh, I think there is. The real problem is how people perceive this challenge. I mean, Max, here, is not going to kill

Palmer. Are you, Max?" asked Tristram.

Max pondered this question a second and then shook his head. "I suppose it would be suicide to kill him, so no, I won't do that, though I may wound the blackguard."

"Right, though not mortally. So what I will do is publish a drawing that shows Palmer as a cat, perhaps a tiger, menacing poor, innocent Philippa, who will be a very pretty little mouse. That should do the trick. In the background, I will put Max, not easily identifiable, except as a man with a dueling pistol or sword."

As he spoke, Tristram drew the picture, and when he was done, both his listeners had to agree that it would probably be enough to defuse the situation Max had created after stealing Kate away from Palmer.

"Very well, my boy. Draw your pictures and see that they are published just as soon as possible. I do not enjoy being the brunt of people's jokes. And as for Max here, I really do not wish to see his chances with Miss Beauchamp ruined. At this point, her father would have every right to pull his consent to the marriage. And you, Max, you had better smooth things over with that girl yourself — only the way you can do it," said the viscount with a leer.

"Then are we to wish you happy, Papa?" asked Max.

"No, pray do not bother. I am not happy, nor am I likely to be so ever again," came the glum reply.

"Cheer up, Papa. Perhaps you can do something to disgust Lady Anne, and she will throw you over for someone else."

"Who else would have her?" said the viscount, reaching for his hat and heading for the door.

When he was gone, Max slouched in the chair, his chin resting on his chest. He watched as Tristram continued to perfect his sketches.

"You are a deep 'un, Tris."

"How so?"

"A year ago, if anyone had told me that it would be you, time and again, who would come up with solutions to our problems, I would have said they were all about in the head. Now I begin to think you are the only one among us who has any sense at all."

"That is kind of you, Max, but I think you exaggerate."

"As you wish, but I thank you for your help in the matter. I wish I could think of some way to repay you."

"The morning paper has arrived, gentlemen," said Barton, entering the room and placing it on a table.

Max leaned forward and turned to the announcements. There it was, the announcement of his forthcoming nuptials to Miss Philippa Beauchamp. His heart sank. It was official now. There was no backing out of it, not with honor.

With a sigh, Max closed the paper and sat back again.

Perhaps he should just let Palmer find his mark.

Kate was almost at the end of her tether. She had gone out riding in the park with her groom until Bobby had protested that Mr. MacAfee would surely think he was shirking his duties at the stable. Finally, she agreed to turn Early Girl back home.

Unfortunately, as they neared the entrance to the park gates, four or five riders rode through the opening, eyeing both her and the mare with wide grins. One of them, a young man named Varner to whom her father had sold a horse, pulled up and greeted her.

"Good morning, Miss O'Connor," said the young man with a nod.

"Hello, Mr. Varner," said Kate, pulling

Early Girl to one side to allow them to pass.

Mr. Varner had other ideas, and said, "Allow me to introduce you to my friends — Mr. Ammons, Lord Westbrook, and Mr. Sellers."

"How do you do, gentlemen?" Seeing that Mr. Varner was intent on keeping her from passing for some reason, Kate asked cordially, "I see you are riding Windswept. Is he behaving himself?"

"What? Oh, yes, a fine horse. And what of you, Miss O'Connor? I could have sworn I saw your father selling that very horse yesterday at Tattersall's. To Mr. Darby, if I recollect properly. How is it you are riding her once again?"

Kate's smile failed to reach her eyes as she said, "I'm sure I don't know anything about that, Mr. Varner. Perhaps it was another of his horses. You know I do not keep up with my father's business."

"Really? That is not what Mr. Palmer was telling us at the club last night after he challenged Mr. Darby to a duel. You must be terribly flattered, Miss O'Connor," he said before tipping his hat and riding away with his friends.

Their raucous laughter filled the air, and Kate kicked her heels against Early Girl's sides and rode quickly home.

After hurrying up to her room, she threw off her habit and changed before going downstairs in search of her father. As usual, he was in the breakfast room with several newspapers spread in front of him.

"Papa! I have just heard the most horrific tale!"

"Here now, Kate, sit down and calm yourself. What is it?"

"It is about Max and Mr. Palmer!"

"The duel, you mean?"

"You knew?"

"Your uncle and I went to his club after the ball and learned of it. It is no affair of yours," he said, returning to his papers.

"No affair of mine?" she cried, pushing his papers away and planting herself in front of him. "Why do you think they are fighting the duel? It is because that . . . that deuced pudding-heart, Palmer . . ."

"Language, young lady," said her father.

". . . has spread the tale of my going to Tattersall's. Max found out and hauled him off the dance floor last night — while I was dancing with the lout!"

"Wait a minute. You went to Tattersall's? After I had told you under no circumstances would I allow a daughter of mine to do such a foolish thing?"

Kate nodded, and her father shook his head, his jaw muscles working furiously as he digested this bit of news. She would be ruined by that alone. Never mind that Darby — a man just betrothed to another — had dragged her name into the dirt by his scandalous behavior at the Lacey ball the night before.

"Papa?" she said softly. "Papa, are you all right? You are white as a ghost. I . . . I'm sorry, Papa."

He shook his head again and looked up at her this time. "What are we to do?"

"I don't know, Papa. I want to talk to Max, to tell him not to be so foolish as to fight a duel over this, but I cannot very well go next door and ask to speak to him. Will you do it for me, Papa? Please!"

Mr. O'Connor patted his daughter's trembling hand and rose. "I'll go. I have a word or two to say to Mr. Darby anyway."

"May I . . ."

"No!" He sighed and continued more gently, "You have to distance yourself from Max. I know you are very fond of him, but he is betrothed to Miss Beauchamp, and each time the two of you are seen together, it will only stir the flames of scandal. I will tell him that you are thinking about him, but that you are wise enough to know you must not see each other. Do you understand, Kate?"

She nodded, tears forming in her eyes, but she would not cry. She simply could not allow herself to do so.

If she started, she was very much afraid she would never be able to stop.

Max took Tristram's advice and danced attendance on his new fiancée day and night for the next few days. He was to be seen in her family's pew at church services on Sunday morning, and every afternoon in the park, driving her around. The fact that Miss Beauchamp looked more miserable with each passing day did little to help in his campaign to stem the tide of gossip, but she did agree to accompany him.

By Monday, with the publication of Tristram's drawings, the Darbys appeared ready to overcome the attendant scandal. The duel, which was to be secret, had been postponed as the weather turned wet and cold. Neither would have kept Palmer or Max from meeting, but their seconds convinced them that the early morning fog would play havoc with the business.

Tuesday, however, dawned clear, and the duel could no longer be postponed. Palmer had spent the previous night drinking toasts to everyone at his club, loudly declaring his intention of killing his man. As a result, the field of honor was a very crowded one with many onlookers.

" 'Tis more like race day at Newmarket," declared Kieran O'Connor to Tristram and Max.

"Your being here, Mr. O'Connor, is only going to convince everyone that Kate is the cause behind this absurd duel," said Max, lifting his pistol and sighting it.

"Nonsense. We are neighbors, and so I have been busily reminding everyone. As far as anyone within the sound of my voice knows, you and Kate are like brother and sister." With a wink, he announced loudly, "Our families have known each other for donkey's years, my boy. Where else should I be but here to support you?"

Max chuckled and clasped the older man's hand. "What the devil is that Irishman going on about?" demanded Lord Tavistoke.

Tristram hissed, "He is trying to smooth things over for our audience." He cocked his head at the growing assemblage of spectators and added, "Shake his hand like a long-lost brother."

"O'Connor!" said the viscount, clapping the other man on the back and smiling widely. "So glad you could come to support our boy in this dirty business. Not that there is any doubt as to the outcome. Everyone who knows Max knows there is no better shot in all of England."

"This is rapidly becoming a blasted circus," grumbled Max. "Tristram, go over there and find out if Palmer is done with his preening."

Tristram hurried away to consult with Osgood, Palmer's second. He returned and said, "He's ready now. Remember, Max, you don't really want to kill him."

"I dashed well do after his telling everybody about this. What was he thinking?"

"Probably that if there is a big enough audience, you will not dare to kill him," said Tris.

"I'm not going to do so," snapped Max.

"Good, and turn your collar up so that there is less of your white shirt showing."

"The man cannot hit the side of a mountain," said Max. "I've seen him shoot at Manton's."

"This isn't Manton's Shooting Gallery," said Tristram, reaching out and rearranging his brother's collar.

The surgeon was standing by. The crowd quieted. Palmer, looking a little pale, walked to the center of the opening where

Max waited calmly. Back to back, they began to walk.

"One . . . two . . . three . . ." Until finally, they reached ten.

Max turned and raised his pistol. Palmer did the same, though his movement was jerky. Max waited, grimacing when Palmer closed his eyes to pull the trigger. The sound was deafening. The ball found its mark in the top of Max's left arm. Palmer let out a squeak of horror. His pistol as steady as ever, Max pointed it up and fired into the air. Senseless, Palmer slipped to the ground while the crowd voiced their approval of Max's action.

The surgeon hurried to Max's side. Barton, who had insisted on accompanying his young masters, was already helping Max out of his coat.

"Sorry, Barton. I'm afraid it is quite ruined."

"I shall have it rewoven, Master Max. Do not trouble yourself."

"How do you feel, my boy?" asked his father.

"How do you think I feel?" he snapped. "Tris, get me to the carriage. I would hate to faint dead away like Palmer."

"Just so," said Tristram, putting his arm around Max and leading him away with the surgeon following.

By the time the surgeon had pronounced it a minor wound and had bandaged it, the clearing was empty. Only O'Connor, the viscount, the surgeon, and the brothers remained.

"Tris, I'm afraid I cannot drive us home. You're going to have to do it."

"Me? Are you trying to make *me* faint?" said the horrified Tristram. "You know my driving skills are almost nil."

O'Connor spoke up and said, "I'll drive you home, Max. Tristram can ride with your father, your servant, and the surgeon. Let me tie my hack to the back of the curricle."

"Thank you, Mr. O'Connor. I was surprised to see you here, but I appreciate your standing by me."

"A pleasure, my boy. You handled that situation just as you ought."

Max smiled and settled onto the seat with a sigh. He had never been shot before. It was not a pleasant sensation. His shoulder was on fire, and the surgeon's mixture of water and laudanum was having its way with him.

"You know, my boy, I am very sorry that you have to wed money. I understand, of course."

"Do you?" murmured Max.

"Yes, one wants to do right by one's family. But it is a shame. You and my Kate would have gotten along famously together, I'm sure of it. As a matter of fact, I think even now she cares more than a little for you, if you do not mind my saying so."

"Hmmmm." Max's head lolled against the Irishman's shoulder, and the only sound to be heard was the jingle of the harnesses and the horses' hooves as they carried them back to London.

Eighteen hours after being shot, Max was restless and ready to resume his life. There was no place to go, however. It was close to midnight, and he had just awakened from his drug-induced sleep. His head hurt from the laudanum and his arm ached, but he was little the worse for wear. Tristram was out, and Barton's constant hovering was driving him mad.

"I am going out," he announced to the servant.

"But, sir, how will you get into a coat with your shoulder hurt? It would be best to wait until tomorrow like the surgeon said."

"I will simply put my arm — ouch! Blast! Help me with this, Barton."

"I will try, Master Max, but do tell me if I hurt you."

"Ouch!" yelped Max. "Oh, devil take it, man. Never mind. I'll go for a stroll in the garden."

"You should wear your greatcoat around your shoulders, sir. It is rather chilly."

"Nonsense! And do stop fussing over me, Barton. I am not a child. Just leave me alone. Go to bed. Go to a tavern. You are dismissed for the night!" barked Max, taking the blanket off his bed, throwing it around his shoulders, and stalking out the door.

Through the drawing room and down the short hall to the garden he marched, coming to rest finally at the small bench beside the garden wall.

Not that he had any hope of a reply, but he called softly, "Iseult? Are you there?"

"Max?" He could hear her moving quickly to the gate and opening it. Then she was in front of him, her anxious gaze searching his face.

"You were wounded," she whispered.

"Only a little," he replied, feeling much more the thing.

"Oh, Max!" she breathed, throwing her arms around his neck. He groaned, and she withdrew in horror. "I have hurt you. I am sorry, Max. Come over here and sit down," she said, picking up the blanket she had knocked off his shoulders and following him to the bench.

When she had gently placed the blanket around his shoulders again, she said, "There. Is that better?"

"No, but this is," he said, turning and taking her into his arms for a breathless kiss that seemed to go on forever.

When he finally drew away, Kate was left smiling contentedly.

Her contentment vanished as Max said, "Kate, I am sorry. I shouldn't have done that."

"I understand," she said, her voice hollow.

Max shook his head and took her hands in his. "No, you don't. I didn't mean . . . devil take me, Kate, I have tried not to think of you, to think of doing that with you, and it is impossible. Knowing you are just next door is torture for me. Do you feel it, too?"

Her smile reappeared, and she nodded, moving closer until she, too, was under the warm wool blanket, resting her head against his broad chest.

"How did we get into this mess? We both know it is impossible," he said, stroking her hair and kissing the top of her red curls.

"There was nothing we could do about it, Max. It was meant to be. Perhaps it is something to keep us warm when we are in our dotage."

"It keeps me warm enough right now," quipped Max, tilting her chin up for a quick kiss on the lips. "Where will it end?"

"It will end when you marry, or perhaps when Papa realizes I am not going to find a husband here in England, and he and Mama finally agree to take me home to Ireland."

"Ireland. That's so very far away," said Max.

Kate kissed his fingers as he toyed with her curls. "It is no farther away than a wedding bed with Miss Beauchamp."

"True, too true."

They were silent for a few minutes. Then Max said, "Are you sure you do not have a wealthy uncle someplace?"

"No, though from the talk Papa heard this morning after he spread it about that our families are well acquainted, I do have some distant cousins who are equally poor. Amazing how a simple lie can be twisted into such a tale," she added with a bitter laugh.

"Amazing," he echoed, tilting her face to meet his. After several moments, he leaned his forehead against her and quipped, "So now we are cousins?"

"Distant cousins," she said, shivering in his arms. He pulled the blanket closer and held her tight against him.

"I like your father," he said suddenly. "He is a man of honor and wisdom."

"Thank you. I like yours, too. You were asleep when my mother and I called to inquire after you, but your father was there. He is quite a charmer, isn't he?"

"When he is not gaming away a fortune," came the dry reply.

"Is he really going to marry Lady Anne Graves?"

"Not if he can escape, he isn't."

"Oh," she said, dropping her gaze again. "I thought . . . well, I should let you go back inside. It cannot be doing your shoulder any good to sit outside in the damp night air."

"I'm fine, really. Stay with me," whispered Max, and she settled into his embrace once again.

"A little while longer," she said, laying her head on his good shoulder again.

Two days later, Tristram entered the

small drawing room wearing a wide smile. Max was seated on the sofa with their father by his side.

"Hello, Papa, I did not expect to find you here," said Tristram.

"Just came to visit Max for a minute."

"Yes, he wanted to know if he was any closer to my marriage settlements," said Max.

"Only Max tells me he ain't interested in setting a date just yet. Very selfish of him, I think," said Viscount Tavistoke.

"Well, never mind about Max's betrothal. Just look at this!" said Tristram, placing a leather purse on the table in front of them.

Max emptied the contents on the table and quickly totaled the coins. Glancing up in bewilderment, he said, "Where did you get all this?"

"Who cares!" said the viscount, picking up the coins and replacing them in the purse.

"Three hundred and twenty-six guineas! Imagine my little novel earning me that kind of money! It's a small fortune!"

"Congratulations, Tris. I am happy for you. What are you going to do with all this?"

"Do? Why, I'm going to invest it," said

Tristram, taking the purse from his father.

"All of it, my boy? You don't want to do that," said the viscount. He reached for the purse again, but Tristram pulled it out of his father's grasp.

"What sort of investments?" asked Max.

"Do you have any idea how much money my publisher is making? And I am only one of his authors. He wants me to be his partner, Max. I could write and work with him, help him find new talent. With my connections, I can get into the literary salons and discover new poets, new novelists. Can you imagine a more perfect life?"

"Not for you, I can't," said Max, smiling at his younger brother's enthusiasm. "So how do you go about being this fellow's partner?"

"First of all, I would not receive any monies for this second novel. And I will probably need to put in some of this purse, as well."

"Not the purse, too," said their father.

"Are you sure that is wise, Tris?" asked Max.

"The two of you need to remember that I am not some sort of child. I am a grown man, and I know what I am doing."

"I did not mean to insinuate that you did not," said Max.

"And I just thought you might want to share with your old father," said the viscount.

"I am sorry, Papa. Not this time," said Tristram.

"Very well, then I am going to leave. If you and Max have any say in the matter, I will probably die a pauper in debtor's prison."

"I thought you were going to wed Lady Anne," said Max.

"If you were a few years younger, lad, I would wash your mouth out with soap! Good day to you, my fine, selfish sons!"

When he was gone, Max said, "Now, back to this business venture of yours. I do not mean to treat you like a child. I only wanted to suggest that you speak to somebody, somebody with experience in business. Heaven knows, I am not the one to consult. I know even less about business matters than I do about love. I am the last one to ask."

"Well, I suppose it couldn't hurt to consult with someone. But who?"

"You could speak to Mr. Beauchamp. He has been very successful in business, though I have no idea what type of business he has."

"A capital idea. I will do that. In the

meanwhile, why don't you and I go out and buy a coat to replace the one that was ruined? I'll buy it. No need to charge it to the marquess this time."

"No, I don't need another coat, Tris. What would be the point? I have already secured my future with Miss Beauchamp."

"Speaking of Miss Beauchamp, have you seen her since the duel?"

"No, I haven't been out since then."

"Are you not a trifle bored?"

"Not really. Actually, I have been reading your novel. It is quite good."

"Oh, uh, thank you, Max. That means a great deal, your reading my work. I really did not expect you to do so. Reading is not your typical pastime."

"But it is your book, Tris. That makes a difference. Now if you'll excuse me, I think I will go to bed and read a little more."

"Oh, of course," said Tristram.

Max slipped into his room and shut the door.

"Are they gone?" asked Kate, stepping out of the shadows.

"Tris is still here, at the desk. I'm afraid he is going to be there for some time."

"But I have to be home soon. Mama was only going to my aunt's house for the morning."

"Don't worry. If he is not gone in half an hour, I will go out there and distract him so that you can slip out unnoticed. Now, where were we?" he asked with a wolfish grin.

"Max, behave yourself," she whispered, laughter bubbling beneath the sound. "We were playing piquet for a penny a point."

"And a kiss for every ten pennies," he said, taking the seat across from hers near the table by the fire.

"Mr. Darby to see you, sir," said the starchy butler.

Robert Beauchamp glanced up, then frowned in surprise. "When my man said Mr. Darby, I assumed it would be your brother, the other Mr. Darby."

"I hope you are not too disappointed, Mr. Beauchamp," said Tristram.

"Not at all. Come in, young man, and have a seat. What can I do for you this afternoon?" asked Mr. Beauchamp, walking around his huge desk and taking a chair near the fire.

"My brother suggested that you might be a good person for me to consult, Mr. Beauchamp. He told me you are very successful in business, and since I am contemplating an investment, he thought it would be a good idea to speak to you."

"An investment, eh? What sort of investment? I dabble in several commodities and other concerns, but I am hardly an expert in all business matters."

"Well, perhaps I should explain first of all. I write novels."

"Indeed? I had no idea. How many have you written?"

"Only two so far, though I will begin my third soon."

"And you want to publish these novels?"

"No, sir. That is, they are already published. Well, the second one should be out in a month or two."

"I am impressed."

"My publisher has offered me a partnership. I am thinking about it."

"I know nothing about the publishing business, Mr. Darby, but I can tell you some of the things I look for when I am considering a new venture. Would that be helpful?"

"Oh, yes, sir. Most helpful."

"Very well. The first thing is, do you trust this publisher?"

An hour later, Mr. Beauchamp was winding up Tristram's lesson when the door opened.

"Excuse me, Papa, but Everman told me

you had company, and I thought I would see if you wanted refreshments. Oh, Mr. Darby. I did not know it was you," said Philippa, blushing perfectly as she told her little lie.

"Good afternoon, Miss Beauchamp," he said formally. "Your father has been kind enough to impart a portion of his business expertise to me."

"Is he a good student?" she asked with a giggle.

"Very good. I like his questions and his quick wits. I think he will make a splendid businessman."

"How wonderful," she said, her blue eyes shining. "So should I tell the footman to bring a tray?"

"I should not take up anymore of your time, sir."

"Nonsense. I have enjoyed myself. Why don't we join Philippa in the drawing room? You two should get better acquainted anyway, since you will soon be related." He did not catch their startled glances as he continued, "How is your brother doing, by the by?"

"He is improving daily. I suspect he will be out and about in a day or two," said Tristram, following his host out of the study and down the long, wide corridor.

Peering over the undersized Beauchamp, he studied Philippa's swishing skirts farther ahead of them, and his heart beat a little faster.

"Good. I do not approve of dueling, but I understand that he conducted himself honorably."

"Very much so," said Tristram.

"The cause . . ."

"Is a private matter, I believe," said Tristram.

"Something about your distant cousin, I think," said Beauchamp, probing a little deeper.

"So I understand," said Tristram.

"Good. I would hate to think it was over something my daughter said. When I saw that ridiculous drawing in the papers, I worried that Philippa's good name might become embroiled in a scandal."

"Not at all, sir. Philippa's good name is quite intact," said Tristram. "Besides, the picture did not take away from her. I thought it enhanced her image of innocence."

"Having one's picture drawn and placed in a newspaper of any sort is hardly likely to enhance one's reputation. But let us not speak of it in front of Philippa," said the proud father. "I kept it away from her."

"Very considerate of you, sir," said Tristram, entering the drawing room and breathing a sigh of relief when he realized Mrs. Beauchamp was not there.

As if reading his mind, Philippa's father said, "My wife has gone to the country for a week or two to visit her, uh, sister."

"Would you care for a cup of tea, Mr. Darby?" asked Philippa.

"Yes, thank you. Sugar only."

"And, Papa, I know how you want yours."

The beauty poured the tea without spilling a drop, the sure sign of a well-trained young lady. The three of them made polite conversation for the next thirty minutes. Finally, Tristram announced that he should be going.

Mr. Beauchamp rose and shook his hand while Tristram thanked him for his help. Philippa shot him a longing look, and smiled when he bowed over her hand.

The butler entered and said, "Pardon me, Mr. Beauchamp, but you wanted to be told when the post arrived. I have placed it in your study."

"Oh, yes. Thank you, Everman. I must go, Mr. Darby. My daughter will see you out," he added, hurrying out of the drawing room.

When he was gone, Philippa let out a
squeak of delight and threw herself into
Tristram's arms.

Nine

"Two days of innocent pleasure, whiling away the hours in the company of the one you love, is more than many people have," said Kate, holding Max's hand as the tears ran down her cheeks.

"Kate, please, do not cry. I cannot bear it."

"I'm sorry," she said with a sniffle.

Forcing a smile to her lips, she willed the tears away. They had promised each other that there would be no regrets, and she was spoiling these last precious moments. Max was well enough to return to Society and to the beautiful Philippa Beauchamp. Their time together was over.

She opened the garden gate. Slipping through it would be the end. She gazed into those deep blue eyes one last time and offered her lips for a final kiss.

"I will always love you, Kate."

"And I will love you, too. I hope you will find a measure of happiness, of peace."

"You, too, my love. Good-bye."

He took her in his arms and kissed her until she thought her heart would burst.

Tearing herself away, Kate slipped through the garden gate and straight into her mother's arms.

"Come into the house, my dear," said Mrs. O'Connor, placing a bracing arm around her daughter's shaking shoulders.

In the privacy of her mother's small sitting room, Kate spilled the tale of the past two days, leaving out many of the intimate details. Her mother listened without questioning her.

When Kate's tears were spent, her mother said, "Do we need to worry about a child?"

Kate's eyes flew to her mother's face and she said, "No! There was nothing like that, Mama! I promise you, Max was a perfect gentleman."

"Perfect?" said Mrs. O'Connor with a knowing smile that made Kate giggle. "Your father was a perfect gentleman, too, but that did not prevent him from kissing me in a manner that . . . well, you know."

Heaving a sigh, Kate said, "Yes, I know, but you married Papa."

She slipped to the floor and placed her head in her mother's lap, as she had done as a little girl. While her mother stroked her hair, she cried more tears for what might have been.

"The date has been set — six weeks from this Saturday morning. I asked her father to arrange with the bishop for a special license, but he said he didn't want to rush his little girl," said Max, plopping down on the sofa and putting his feet on the table in front of him.

Tristram swiveled in his chair to stare at his brother. "Personally, I think six weeks is hasty enough, especially since I thought you were trying to get to know Miss Beauchamp better."

"What is the point? With my fiancée, time is irrelevant. She cannot manage to say more than a word or two to me at a time. That was why I wanted to get it over with. We can become acquainted on our wedding night," said Max, his voice devoid of anticipation.

"On your . . . the devil you say! I think you've got windmills in the head, Max."

"What makes you so heated?" demanded Max.

"What . . . you, that's what! You are marrying this girl without knowing anything about her. What are her likes, her dislikes? And does she have anything to say in the matter?"

"How should I know? I left it to her father to inform her," said Max. "What do you care, Tris? You're going into the publishing business. A good thing, too, since Mr. Beauchamp has assured me that the marriage settlements will not be paid until after the nuptials. After that, you can take your share and buy all the ink and paper your presses can hold. Then Papa can pay the marquess all that he owes him, and Monty and Clarissa can fix up the Hall."

"And you?"

"Me? The devil may take me and all of Beauchamp's money, too!"

"Damn the money, Max! I'm thinking about you. You and Miss O'Connor. What happens to Kate when you have wed Miss Beauchamp?"

"Keep Kate out of this," snarled Max, his indifference replaced by anger.

"Why? Doesn't the woman you love have any say in the matter of your wedding? And don't deny that she hasn't been here almost every minute since you were wounded in that silly duel."

"I'm not asking for your blessing, Tris. I'm doing this for you and Papa and Monty, so shut up and say thank you!"

"Thank you for ruining your life? You selfish . . . deceitful . . . bah!" Tristram slammed out of the room.

"Of all the ungrateful prigs," said Max, throwing a small vase against the wall. With a grunt of satisfaction, he, too, left the house.

Max walked to his club with the intention of drowning his sorrow. He did not usually resort to such a cowardly exploit, but he was beyond caring. All he wanted was to dull the pain and quell the panic in his breast every time he thought of wedding the quiet Miss Beauchamp instead of his beloved Kate.

No matter how many times he told himself it was not just the money, he could not find peace. It was also a matter of honor. He had pledged himself to Miss Beauchamp, and Miss Beauchamp he would wed. It was the right thing, the honorable thing.

"Bring a large port," he told the footman. "Make it two."

"Nursing more than that flesh wound, Darby?" asked Osgood, sitting down across the table from him and shuffling a deck of cards.

"None of your business," said Max. The footman produced the two glasses. After downing one, Max sipped the other more slowly.

"Women, eh? What chance do we stand with them?"

"Better than without them, I suppose," said Max.

Osgood laid out a game of patience and played at it with lackluster interest.

"The red ten on the black knave," said Max. "There," he added, pointing to the spot.

"My sister is forever after me to marry," said Osgood. "I have decided it just isn't worth it. I mean, look at you and Palmer. Until those two females got in the way, you didn't have anything against each other."

"Actually, we did. I did not approve of his horsemanship. The man's a ham-fisted clunch when it comes to horses. It goes against all my sensibilities," quipped Max.

Osgood collected his cards and began shuffling again. "A game of piquet?" he asked.

"Why not? What stakes?"

"A shilling a point?"

"You're on," said Max, his mind on Kate and the kisses they had shared as stakes. He finished the second glass and ordered two more.

Two hours later, Max rose from the table. He handed Osgood his scribbled vowel. With unsteady steps, he made his way home, cursing himself as he walked.

Max had always prided himself on his unwavering good sense. Though he had wagered on horse races when he himself was riding, that had been different. He had always been certain of the outcome. He had never gambled with money he did not possess.

As he staggered into the house, he was hit by the realization that he was no better than his father. Going into his bedroom, Max became violently ill.

When he had finished being sick, he threw himself onto the bed and promptly passed out.

"I have something here that will make you feel better, Master Max," said Barton, helping Max rise up on one elbow.

"What is it?" came the gravelly voice.

"Just something to help settle your stomach, sir. It's a secret, and if I told you what it contained, it might make you sick all over again. There, that's good," said the servant.

"What time is it?"

"It is one o'clock in the afternoon, sir. A letter arrived for you, if you would care to read it now."

"Yes, hand it over," said Max, sitting up

on the side of the bed and waiting for his head to stop throbbing.

He looked at the feminine handwriting and tore it open eagerly. His face crumbled as he read Kate's words.

My Dearest Max,

I must write to tell you that my father has agreed to take me home. We will be closing up the house and leaving at the beginning of the week. I could not leave without telling you how much I have enjoyed our time together. I will always remember you with fondness and with gratitude, too, for saving Early Girl for me. Know that I will always stand . . .

> *Your friend,*
> *Kate*

"Hell and blast!" muttered Max, tossing the letter toward the fire. Immediately repentant, he jumped up to retrieve it, putting out the smoldering corner with his fingers.

His head still throbbing, he put the note away before staggering into the drawing room and calling, "Barton! Draw me a bath!"

An hour later, bathed, combed, and

dressed, Max waited for his brother to return. He hated the thought of asking Tristram for some of his hard-earned money, but he had no choice. A debt of honor had to be repaid instantly. He knew that Philippa's father would probably advance him the sum against the settlements, but he was loath to ask such a favor.

Finally, Tristram entered the house, whistling like he had not a care in the world.

"Good morning, Max," he said.

"Good morning, Tris. I need to speak to you."

"Oh? Well, let me get out of this greatcoat first. Thank you, Barton," he said to the servant as he removed the heavy coat. "Now, what is it?"

"I . . . I will not try to sugarcoat it, and I give you leave to ring a peal over me, but I need to borrow ninety-eight guineas to pay a debt."

"Surely a tradesman can wait another few weeks until the marriage settlements have been paid," said Tristram.

"It is not a tradesman. It is a gambling debt." Max faced his brother squarely, although he wished he might melt through the floor.

"Gambling? You? I cannot believe it!"

exclaimed Tristram. "Not you, Max. You never gamble — except with your horses, but that is not the same."

"Precisely, but I'm afraid, after our argument, I went out last night to drown my sorrows, and I met Osgood. Before I knew it, an hour or so of piquet had passed, and I was ninety-eight guineas short. I really do hate to ask, Tris. . . ."

"I don't mind your asking, Max, but I simply don't have it. I told you I was going to invest that money, and so I have. I kept only forty guineas. I'm sorry."

"Ah well, never mind, then. It is my problem. I shall have to ask Mr. Beauchamp to advance me the money."

"Do you think you should? What if he wants to cancel the betrothal?" asked Tristram, his eyes glowing strangely.

Max took this as a sign of his brother's concern and patted him on the shoulder as he passed by.

"Then he will cancel it. I have nowhere else to turn. I'll be diddled if I'll go to the marquess. One of us in his debt is enough."

"You sound like you would not mind having the betrothal canceled," said Tristram.

"Perhaps I wouldn't," murmured Max.

"Max, if you dislike the idea of marrying Philippa so much, why don't you just break the demmed engagement?"

"You know a gentleman cannot do that. It would have to come from her or her father. Besides, we both know I have to go through with it because of the money. And that brings us back full circle. Where am I to get so much money?"

"I have an idea, Max. There is another possibility, a way of getting your hands on the marriage settlements a little faster."

"I'm listening," said Max.

"We will take Miss Beauchamp on a little picnic in the country tomorrow, only we will not return. We'll continue north until we reach Gretna Green, where you can marry over the anvil."

"Impossible! She will never agree to the scheme."

"I think she will, once she gets used to the idea."

Max frowned and shook his head, until Tristram demanded, "Do you have a better idea? No? Then we do it my way." He rose and fetched paper and pen. "Here, write her a note inviting her on the picnic."

Max grumbled as he wrote, and Tristram said, "Only think, in a couple of days, you'll be a married man."

"Shaddup," said Max, sealing the envelope.

"Good, now I will deliver it personally. You stay here and try to behave."

"Do not order me about. I can still wrestle you to the ground, halfling."

"If you can catch me," laughed Tristram, hurrying out the door.

Max spent the remainder of the afternoon nursing his sore head. Though he was tempted to go next door and pay the O'Connors a visit, he controlled this impulse. He had already done enough damage, trifling with Kate's affection. Not that he had not trifled with his own, for he had. He was positively blue deviled without her.

Taking out some dice, he played against himself to divert his thoughts. He was less than successful with this gambit. With every roll of the dice, he became more and more down pin. Finally, he threw the dice across the table and left them there. Rising, he began to pace like one of the tigers at the Exchange.

He was not like Tristram, he told himself. It did not take much to make him happy. Tristram, on the other hand, had always had the soul of a poet. He felt things deeply. For Max, as long as he could be

276

free to ride a horse, he had been content.

Suddenly, this was not enough. Given a choice between Thunderlight and Kate, he would chose Kate — amazing as this was to him. Kate. His heart ached to see her and hold her, to make her his own, but he could see no way out of marrying Miss Beauchamp.

When he thought of Philippa Beauchamp, Max wondered what had attracted him to her in the first place. She was beautiful, in a very ordinary way. Mostly, he had to admit, it had been her father's money that had caught his attention.

But now it simply wasn't enough.

Max paused in his pacing. It was like a great light had been lit. Without pausing to think what he would say, he rushed through the door and outside, striding purposefully down the pavement to the O'Connors' front door and rapping a lively tattoo.

"I want to see Miss O'Connor. It is urgent!"

"One moment, sir, I will see . . . sir, please . . ."

In two great steps, Max was at the drawing room door, pushing it open and entering while the butler bobbed along on his heels, protesting volubly.

The wind was knocked quite out of his chest when he realized the room was in Holland covers. Stopping so suddenly, the butler ran into him and then backed away.

Whirling around, Max grabbed the servant by the collar and demanded, "Where are they? Do not tell me they have already gone!"

"No, sir, they are still packing. Allow me to see if Miss O'Connor will receive you."

"Very well, but tell her who has called, and that it is urgent."

"I shall, sir."

The butler hurried away, and Max tore the cover off the sofa, but he didn't sit down. Instead, he resumed his pacing.

A moment later, he stopped, tears filling his eyes when he spied Kate smiling at him from the doorway. Without a word, he hurried to her side, took her into his arms, and kissed her — again and again, with a hunger that reached his very soul.

Taking his lips from hers, he kissed her eyes, her forehead, burying his face in her hair, murmuring her name over and over.

Finally, a foolish smile on his face, he closed the door and led her to the sofa, pulling her onto his lap, and taking her face in his hands.

"Kate, my dearest Kate. I could not stay away any longer. I love you as I have never loved anything or anyone. I cannot bear the thought of living if you will not consent to be my wife. Please, Kate, say you will marry me."

She gazed into his eyes, smiling and nodding. "Yes, yes, Max. It is what I want more than anything."

This pronouncement caused another bout of kisses and embraces that lasted much longer than propriety dictated, but neither participant seemed to care.

Their breathing ragged, they parted. Kate moved to one side of the sofa and Max to the other, facing each other.

"Max, how will we ever manage this? You are engaged to Miss Beauchamp."

"I know," he said, shaking his head dolefully. "We must think of something. I . . . Kate, I did a stupid thing last night. I gambled and lost, just like my father. I had always sworn . . . but there, I was not myself."

"Oh, Max. How much?"

"Almost one hundred guineas. Not a fortune, but it might as well be to me."

Kate smiled and leaned forward, grasping his hand and kissing it. "Wait here. I'll be right back."

A moment later, she returned, carrying her reticule.

"Max, I know you would not normally accept this, but since that race was your idea in the first place, I want you to have it. Papa told me to keep the extra one hundred fifty guineas. Here," she said, thrusting a bundle of notes at him. "You are sure one hundred will be enough?"

"Kate, I cannot," he said, handing it back.

"Maxwell Darby, do not be stupid. You have just asked me to marry you. What is mine is yours. Do you intend to begin our life together in debtor's prison?"

He chuckled. "I do not think Osgood would do that to me."

"But would it not be better to begin without that hanging over our heads?" she said sensibly.

He took the notes and put them in his pocket, saying simply, "Thank you, Kate."

"You're welcome. Now there is only one thing standing in our way."

Max groaned and ran his fingers through his dark hair. "Miss Beauchamp. And Tristram. Oh, Kate, I let Tristram talk me into a very foolish plan just a little while ago."

"What is it?"

Max outlined Tristram's plan for him and Philippa to elope so that he could receive the marriage settlements sooner.

"Now I not only have to tell her I am not taking her on a blasted picnic, but that I am also ending the betrothal."

"But, Max, surely she will understand," said Kate.

"Will she? I have the distinct feeling that Miss Beauchamp is much more like her mother than anyone knows. She could very well drag both our names through the mud. Mine I don't care about, but yours . . . I'll not have it, Kate."

"Why don't I come along on the picnic tomorrow? When she sees how much we love each other, surely she will not raise a fuss."

"One can only hope," said Max, stroking her fingertips. With a sudden wide grin, he said, "Perhaps you should pack a valise, Kate. It would be a shame for Tristram's plan to be wasted."

"You mean we should elope?" she whispered.

"Would it be so terrible? The thought of waiting weeks until the banns are read is not very appealing, is it? What do you say?"

She smiled, nodding eagerly, and he took

her hand and brought it to his lips for a chaste kiss. He dared not pull her into his arms. He wasn't certain he had the willpower to stop again.

After a moment of gazing into each other's eyes, the pragmatic Kate straightened and said, "Max, I hate to ask, but are you sure you wish to throw away Miss Beauchamp's fortune? I mean, she is her father's only child. You will be wealthy beyond your wildest dreams if you . . . marry . . . oh, Max."

So much for willpower!

The next morning dawned clear and bright. Max had ordered the marquess's landaulet for ten o'clock. Needham, the marquess's head groom, had agreed to drive it. He was a trustworthy servant, so Max was not worried about gossip being carried back to London about their exploits. He was not at all certain what Miss Beauchamp's reaction would be — tears, screaming, or quiet acceptance. At any rate, the last thing he wanted was someone reporting every detail to the scandal sheets.

Tristram eyed the landaulet with trepidation. "Max, I don't like these things. Are you sure Needham can drive this?"

"Upon my honor, Tris, you know he can. He drives at least as well as I do."

"All right, all right. I just don't fancy being turned over and being forced to ride one of these jittery beasts to the nearest inn."

"No need t' worry, Master Tristram," said Needham from the driver's box. "I wouldna let you ride one of 'em anyway."

Tristram grinned at the cheeky groom and said, "So long as we understand each other!"

"I will be back in a minute," said Max, hurrying into the house and coming out with three boxes. Opening the boot of the carriage, he stowed all of these away.

"What was all that?" asked Tristram.

"It was just a few things for the picnic," said Max. Lowering his voice for his brother's ears alone, he added, "And my clothes. You don't want me to go all the way to Scotland wearing the same kit, do you?"

"No, no, of course not. I cannot believe you are really going through with it," said Tristram.

"Do I have a choice?" said Max, trying to keep his face grim, but finding it impossible.

Frowning, Tristram said, "What is so

funny? If I did not know better, I would think you were happy about this."

"Let us say I have reconciled myself to wedding over the anvil. I'll go get Kate."

"I still don't know why you wanted to bring her along," grumbled Tristram.

"And I told you I think it will help Miss Beauchamp accept the matter more quickly. As a matter of fact, with Kate's help, I hope Miss Beauchamp will embrace the idea!"

Whistling, Max trotted next door and up the front steps. Moments later, Kate appeared on his arm, smiling sunnily. She wore a green carriage dress with a fitted spencer that was trimmed in gold braid. Her bonnet was velvet with matching gold braid.

"Good morning, Kate. You are looking very pretty this morning."

"Why, thank you, Tristram. Isn't this the finest weather for a picnic? I cannot wait to leave London behind and get into the country. I understand you have been to this inn before. There are tables outside?"

"What? Oh, yes, along a small stream. It is an idyllic setting," he replied, helping her into the carriage.

Their next stop took them to the Beauchamp town house. Max, once again, trotted up the steps to fetch his fiancée, who wore a rose-colored carriage dress with knots of silk roses pinned here and there. On her bonnet was a huge silk rose that cast her face into shadow.

Max took the box she carried and placed it in the boot before opening the door to the carriage.

Looking inside, he said, "Tristram, I do not want you getting ill. You sit in the forward-facing seat with Miss Beauchamp. Kate and I will manage quite well in the rear-facing seat."

"Are you sure you want me to do that, Max?" asked Tristram. Leaning down and whispering, he said, "Wouldn't it be better for you to sit beside your fiancée?"

"Not at all. Just do as I say," said Max, helping Miss Beauchamp into the carriage as the other two occupants greeted her cordially.

"Now, is everybody settled?" he asked when he had taken the seat beside Kate.

They all agreed that they were, and he gave Needham the office to start. Miss Beauchamp's parasol went up to guard her face from the sun, but Kate threw back her head and laughed at the sheer pleasure of the day to come.

As they drove along in the open carriage,

conversation was limited because of the noise of the road. Max leaned close to Kate and whispered in her ear.

"If I didn't know better, I would guess that those two knew each other as well as we know each other."

"Max, what a thing to say about the girl you were supposed to marry. I'm sure their conversation is perfectly innocent," whispered Kate, smiling at Tristram when he happened to look away from Miss Beauchamp.

An hour later, they arrived at a small posting inn outside London. Most of the traffic that stopped there consisted of people too weary to go on, or those from London who merely wanted a taste of the country.

While the Darby brothers helped the ladies to alight, Needham opened the boot and began hauling out boxes.

"What are you doing?" asked Max.

"I thought these were for your picnic, Master Max," said the groom.

"No, no, not at all. My brother has sent ahead and ordered our nuncheon. Leave those boxes alone."

"I beg your pardon, sir," said the groom before walking away and muttering to himself about the eccentricity of the quality.

"Shall we, ladies?" he said, offering his arm to Kate, who was closest to him. Tristram and Max's fiancée were left to follow.

"Good morning, Mr. Darby. I received your note with your requirements," said the landlord. "You'll find a nice table all laid out for you. Come right this way."

The landlord led them through the inn's public rooms and out a doorway to the back. Following a gravel path, he continued to the stream where a table with a pristine white cloth waited for them. The table was set for four with four chairs. A few paces away, a large blanket was spread on the ground in case anyone wanted to lounge about.

"I have your champagne chilling, sir, and your luncheon will be served in a few minutes." The landlord bowed and left them.

"You seem to have thought of everything, Tristram."

"What a charming place," said Kate, allowing Max to seat her.

Max then took the chair next to her, leaving Tristram to perform the same duty for Miss Beauchamp.

The landlord reappeared with a young man carrying a heavy tray. Balancing the tray on the edge of their table, the landlord served them roasted fowl, sweet peas, and baked pears. He sent the boy back for glasses of cider for the ladies and ale for the gentlemen. All this was accomplished with great style. After a final inspection, he nodded and bowed before leaving them in solitude.

Max opened his mouth to speak, then snapped it shut, unable to think how to begin.

"Food first, I think," he said, making Miss Beauchamp giggle nervously. Max glanced at Kate, but she appeared as puzzled by this as he was. With a shrug, he fell to eating the excellent repast.

After the second remove, the landlord and the lad returned again. This time, the tray contained apples, pears, and a variety of cheeses. It also had the promised champagne and four glasses.

"Would you care to open it, sir?" he asked Tristram. Tristram waved it away, and the landlord performed this office, filling the four glasses and again leaving them alone.

Max raised his glass and said, "To love."

Miss Beauchamp and Tristram both looked surprised, but they raised their glasses and then drank the sparkling liquid.

"To marriage," said Tristram, and the others echoed this sentiment.

Max placed his glass on the table. Tristram did the same.

"Miss Beauchamp, I'm afraid we have gotten you here under false pretenses," said Max.

"Not exactly false, my dear," said Tristram, covering her small hand with his.

Max frowned at the gesture. He glanced at Kate and was relieved to see that she was frowning, too. He was not the only one who was confused.

"Max," said Tristram. "We have a confession to make."

"We?"

"Yes, Philippa and I. I'm afraid I have not been very honorable in all this. When I said we should take Philippa on a picnic so that the two of you could elope, I really meant so that she and I could elope. That is why she brought a bandbox with her."

"The devil you say!" exclaimed Max, thumping the table with his palm. He steadied it as the glasses began to tremble.

"Tris, are you saying that you . . . and Miss Beauchamp . . ." said Kate.

"Yes, though we never meant for it to happen," said Tristram, glancing at the girl by his side. "Philippa is too noble. She would have wed you no matter what, Max. She did not wish to disappoint her father."

"As good a reason as I had," muttered Max.

"You are not too angry with me, are you, Mr. Darby?" asked Philippa Beauchamp, her blue eyes wide with fear.

Max began to laugh. Kate joined him, and soon they were almost falling out of their chairs with amusement.

After a moment, Tristram said, "It is not as funny as all that."

Max held up his hand while he got his mirth under control. When he could speak again, he said, "But it is, Tris. I had decided to call it quits with Miss Beauchamp. I'm sure you will not be offended by that, Miss Beauchamp."

"Not at all," she said, her dimples showing. "And I think it is time you called me Philippa. Tristram has been doing so for ages."

"Thank you, Philippa. I deem it an honor. And you must call me Max, under the circumstances. And this is Kate, to you, since you will be sisters, of sorts."

"So you and Miss O'Connor — I mean, Kate — are to be wed, too?" asked the girl.

"Yes, as soon as we can reach Scotland. I suppose the two of you will go back to

London and tell Philippa's father what happened. I do not envy you that, Tris. is not the sort of man one wants to cros Very powerful friends, he has."

"Oh, Papa is a pussycat. He would not mind."

"Perhaps not, but Philippa and I have decided not to wait, either. We are for the border, too. You will not mind the company, I hope."

"Not at all," said Max, placing an arm around Kate's waist. "The more the merrier."

"Having the two of you along will make things easier, really," said Kate, slapping his hand away. "Philippa, you and I can share a room at each of the inns. Everything will be quite proper."

"Oh, what a splendid idea. That was the one thing I worried about. I love my dear Tristram, but I did not wish to . . . well, you know," said the girl, turning a charming shade of pink.

Max raised his glass again and said, "To us!"

Ten

It was a merry journey indeed. Though there were many stolen kisses, the young ladies managed to keep their swains at bay for the three-day journey. Nor were they overtaken by any angry papas in hot pursuit, since the girls had sent home letters explaining their impetuous flight.

Kate and Max were deliriously happy just spending every waking moment together. As they changed from one traveling coach to the next, they rode side by side, their heads together, discussing their future.

"You will love Ireland, Max. It is so beautiful there."

"I know I will as long as you are there," he whispered.

Kate blushed at the compliment, and said, "I thought Tris was supposed to be the poet in the family."

"Perhaps being with you brings out the poet in me," he said, giving her hand, which he held in his lap, a squeeze.

Snow was falling when they reached

their destination, lending their wedding fairy-tale quality. Forgetting to breat Max had to lean on Tristram for suppo when Kate walked into the chapel.

"You are so beautiful," he whispered when she took his hand.

The short service ended with a kiss. Tristram again was pressed into service to whisper into his brother's ear that they needed to wait until later for that.

Tristram and Philippa were next. Max watched her approach to the altar with wonder. Where, he wondered, was the shy, stumbling girl he had tried to court? In Tristram's company, she was not only beautiful, she was self-possessed and confident.

When the second ceremony was over, the four of them hurried back to the inn, where they had taken two rooms, this time as couples. The landlord and his wife made a living by catering to eloping couples, and they set out a huge feast for the four newlyweds.

"Max, this is wonderful. Have a bite," said Kate, offering her fork to her husband. He took a bite of the rabbit and nodded.

"Who would have thought the Scots could cook like this," he said.

The landlady walked in with another

er, this one containing delicate pas-
es. Max groaned and put his hand on his
omach.

"Ye must try a little, Mr. Darby, or you'll
hurt my feelings, you will."

"I would not want to do that, Mrs.
Brown. Very well, just a little. Here, Kate.
Where are Tristram and Philippa?"

"Oh, they went upstairs fifteen minutes
or more since," said the landlady.

Max chuckled and rose. "We'll take a
couple of your pastries up with us, Mrs.
Brown. I didn't realize it had grown so
late."

The landlady laughed and left them
alone.

Kate slapped at Max's arm and said,
"You are not very subtle, husband."

"If you wanted subtle, you should not
have married me, Kate. I'm too direct in
my dealings. For instance, Tristram might
quote you poetry, but for me, I'll just say,
would you like to go upstairs, Mrs.
Darby?"

"I thought you would never ask," she replied with a giggle.

He caught her to him and gave her a
quick kiss. "A promise of things to
come," he whispered. Taking her hand,
he led her out of the private parlor and

up the stairs to their room.

"I want you to know, my love," he w..
pered as he closed the door. "I don't wr
to frighten you. I know this will be strang
for you, and . . ."

Kate turned and threw her arms around
his neck, molding her body to his. After a
moment, she leaned back in his arms and
giggled. "Don't be absurd, Max. You are
talking to a country girl. I only hope I
don't frighten you."

"Minx!"

"Rogue!"

The two couples had agreed to spend
three days in Scotland, at the Browns' inn.
Though they had planned to meet for
meals each day, they never saw each other
until it was time to board the coach for
home.

Though none of them offered to share
information about their experiences, it was
obvious from their contented smiles that
they were quite happy with their new
mates.

"I shall be glad to get home," said
Philippa. "I do hope Papa is not too
upset."

"I'm sure Tristram will be able to win
him over," said Max. "What about you,

Are you worried that your parents have me horsewhipped?"

"Not Papa. I think he will be secretly pleased. And Mama will be delighted. They married for love, too, you know."

Max insisted on accompanying Tristram and Philippa into the house. As they climbed the steps of the mansion, he explained in an undertone to Kate, "It is the least I can do after jilting his daughter."

"Perhaps, but I am anxious to get home, too," said Kate, pursing her lips at him.

"Don't worry. We will not stay any longer than is necessary," he whispered.

"Papa! Papa!" called Philippa, sweeping past the butler with a smile.

"Philippa!" said Mr. Beauchamp, hurrying into the great hall from the back of the house where his study was located. "My dear child. I should take you over my knee, you know."

The short man favored his new son-in-law with a hard look. Glancing back at his daughter, he asked, "Are you happy, pet?"

"More than I can say," she breathed, releasing her father and holding out her hand to pull Tristram to her side.

Mr. Beauchamp's face softened, and he

extended his hand. "Then I will welco.... him into the family."

"Thank you, sir."

"I told you we should not have come inside," whispered Kate.

Her words caused Beauchamp to look beyond his daughter and her new husband, and his frown returned.

"Darby, you are a very lucky man."

"In what way?" said Max, stepping closer.

"If my daughter were not so happy, I would do my best to have you shot. As it is, you seem to have done her a favor by throwing her over. She never smiled like that about marrying you."

Max chuckled and grasped the hand the older man offered. "I'm glad you see it that way, sir. What's more, Philippa was the one who told me she preferred my brother. I was relieved that she was so sensible."

"Is that right? And you must be the other new Mrs. Darby," said Beauchamp, turning to Kate. "You, too, appear quite content, so I suppose there is nothing else to be said. Unless you would all like to come into the drawing room for a celebratory drink?"

"Not us, Mr. Beauchamp, though we thank you for your gracious offer. I want to

back to my own parents. I know you'll
ıderstand."

"Certainly. We will do that another time,
perhaps at the ball I am holding tomorrow
night to announce Philippa's marriage to
Tristram." He gave a little laugh and said,
"I thought it would be the best way to
spike the guns of the gossips. We can announce yours, too, if you like."

"That would be wonderful," said Max.
"Good-bye, Tris. I'll see you later. Good-
bye, Philippa."

Their farewells made, Max and Kate returned to the carriage. Kate fidgeted with
the strings of her reticule, but otherwise
she remained calm.

Max closed his hand over hers and said,
"You know they will not be too angry. I
may not have money, but I do know
horses. I'll do all I can to help your father
in his business."

"I know, and that will win him over, but
I am still a little nervous. I suppose it is
only right, since I have not been nervous
about anything else over the past week and
a half — since the moment you proposed
to me."

He stole another kiss as the carriage
rolled to a stop.

"Here we go," he said, hopping down

and reaching up to help her.

Before they could turn around, the front door opened and Kate's parents appear. hurrying down the steps to throw the arms around their beloved daughter.

"Darby!" said Mr. O'Connor, his expression fierce. Then he grinned and took Max's hand, shaking it and clapping him on the shoulder.

Mrs. O'Connor stood on tiptoe to kiss his cheek before leading the way inside.

When the celebrating was over at the O'Connor house, Max took his wife home. When they entered the modest house, Barton greeted them with a bottle of champagne and a cold collation.

"I do apologize, Master Max, but since I couldn't know what time you would be arriving home, I could not plan a hot meal for you."

"Think nothing of it, Barton. This is wonderful, isn't it, Kate?"

"Just perfect, Barton."

"I am glad it meets your approval, madam. May I offer my sincerest congratulations and best wishes?"

"Thank you, Barton," said Max. "Oh, and Barton, Tris asked me to tell you that he hopes you will consider being butler to and his new wife."

"Oh, Master Max, I don't know what to
."

"You say yes, that's what you say. No
more toadying to the dirty marquess. You
will have your own household to run, your
own staff to order about . . ."

"As wonderful as it will be, Master Max,
it will not compare to the pleasure I have
had serving you and your brothers."

"Well, thank you, Barton," said Max.
Holding out his hand, he added, "We
never would have succeeded without your
guidance. You know that, don't you?"

Barton looked at the offered hand, hesitating only a moment before grasping it for
a firm shake.

"Thank you, Master Max. That means a
. . . great deal . . . to me. Pardon me," he
said, hurrying out of the room as his emotions got the best of him.

"I feel like it is my first ball," said Kate.
Dropping her necklace, she said, "Oh,
drat."

"I'll get it," said Max, picking up the
necklace and putting it around her neck.
He fastened the clasp and kissed the back
of her neck for good measure.

"None of that," she said with a sigh, "or

300

we will never make it to Mr. Beauchamp's ball."

"Very well, my little shrew."

"I wonder how he put it together so quickly," she mused.

"Knowing Robert Beauchamp, I would say he did it without mussing his cravat. The man is remarkable. When Tris came by to pick up his clothes, he told me that Beauchamp had already set up accounts for both him and Philippa. He has also scouted out a couple of likely estates so they may have their choice."

Looking over her husband's shoulder as he tied his cravat, Kate said, "That could have been you, my love. Any regrets?"

Their eyes met in the glass, and he smiled. Turning his head, he kissed her nose. Then she tumbled into his embrace and their toilettes were forgotten as they found their way to the bed once more.

"I think all of London is here," said Mrs. O'Connor. "How on earth did he manage to put all of this together?"

Not waiting for a reply, she turned to greet her sister. Leading her forward, she said, "Max, you have met my sister, Lady Murray, have you not?"

"Yes, briefly. I attended your ball earlier

in the Season, my lady."

"Did you, my boy? I should have remembered that, you being such a handsome rogue. I do hope you will look after our Kate as she deserves."

"He certainly will, aunt," said Kate, linking arms with her new husband. "Speaking of looking after me, I think the musicians are striking up a waltz."

Taking his cue, Max asked, "Will you do me the honor, Mrs. Darby?"

"I would be delighted," said Kate, strolling onto the floor of the ballroom.

He took her in his arms, only a little closer than propriety dictated, and they set off, in perfect step with one another.

"Have I told you tonight that you are the most beautiful lady at the ball? No one can hold a candle to you with those green eyes."

She gurgled with laughter and said, "It is only right, since you are the most splendid gentleman here tonight. I think you should always wear a blue waistcoat to match your eyes."

He rewarded her with a dizzying twirl that made her giddy. At that moment, Tristram and Philippa whirled by, their gazes locked, oblivious to their surroundings.

"Is that how we look?" asked Kate.

"Certainly not," said Max. "We are much happier than they are."

"I don't know how happy they are, Max, but I could not be happier."

"What about Ireland? Would going home to Ireland make you happier?"

"No, it is no longer as important as it was before. I will be content wherever we are, as long as we are together." She blushed under the warmth of his gaze. "What is it?"

Max shook his head and said, "Nothing. I was just thinking how lucky I am, and how very stupid I almost was."

"That makes two of us," she whispered.

The music ended a few minutes later, and Max and Kate found themselves beside Tristram and Philippa. When the next set started, they switched partners and joined one of the squares forming.

Their gaiety was remarked by all, and rumors were rampant throughout the large gathering. Mr. Beauchamp would say nothing, only smile and wink when anyone asked him about his daughter and her fiancé.

After the quadrille was over, Robert Beauchamp gathered all four of the newly-weds together and herded them onto the small dais he had had constructed for his grand announcement.

A hush settled over the crowd as the musicians played a fanfare to gain their attention.

"My lords, ladies, and gentlemen. I feel like I have done this before," said Beauchamp, sparking a rash of laughter. "But I must tell you, there are different players in this piece tonight, and I could not be happier, because my beloved Philippa is happy at last.

"I know most of you were present when I announced the betrothal of Philippa to Mr. Darby — Mr. Maxwell Darby. I was delighted at the prospect of calling Max my son, but love has a way of changing things. I am here tonight to announce the marriage of my daughter Philippa to Mr. Darby — Mr. Tristram Darby."

Gasps rippled through the spectators. Mr. Beauchamp held up his hands for silence, though it took several seconds to attain.

"That is not all the news," he said. "Mr. O'Connor has given me permission to make another announcement tonight. This one concerns his lovely daughter, Katherine O'Connor, who has just become the bride of Mr. Maxwell Darby."

This was greeted by polite applause, though some of the younger men shouted, "Huzzah! Huzzah!"

Champagne was being passed around, and Mr. Beauchamp raised his glass. "To the happy couples!"

Everyone lifted their glasses and then proceeded to drink.

Suddenly, there was a shout from the entrance of the ballroom. "Married? What do you mean, married?"

Viscount Tavistoke shook off the hands of well-wishers and slogged his way through the crowd to the platform.

"It's a lie, Beauchamp! My boy didn't marry the O'Connor girl. Max, tell him he's made a mistake!" shouted the viscount.

At that moment, the dropping of a pin could have been heard amongst the onlookers. Every eye was glued to the platform.

"Tell him, Max!" cried the viscount, almost in tears.

"Papa, it's true. I married Kate, not Philippa."

"Well, thank heavens one of us was man enough to bite the bullet," growled the viscount, glaring at his son and new daughter-in-law.

"What are you talking about, Papa?" asked Max.

"Me, that's what! I leave it to my sons to repair the family fortunes and what happens? Nothing, nothing at all! But I didn't shrink from my duty. You may thank me. Yes, both of you may thank me!"

"What for, Papa?" asked Tristram.

"For marrying Lady Anne this morning, that's what!"

"Congratulations, Papa!" said both Darby boys.

"A wise man," said Max, a smile playing on his lips. "Lady Anne will be the making of you, Papa. No more late nights, drinking, and gaming. Yes, you'll be much better off with Lady Anne to look after you."

"Yes, well, as I said, somebody had to sacrifice." The viscount looked down and blinked twice when he saw his new wife glaring at him.

"By the way, Papa, my marrying Kate was not the only news," said Max. Pulling Tristram and Philippa forward, he said, "I think you came in too late to hear the other announcement. Tris and Philippa were also married. Isn't that good news?"

"Tristram, my boy!" said the viscount, slapping his youngest son on the back and kissing Philippa on the cheek.

Suddenly, his smile faded, and his face turned a pasty white. Grasping Max's hand to steady himself, he howled, "You mean I did not have to marry Lady Anne after all? Hell and bl . . . ouch! That hurt!" Reeling from the blow of Lady Anne's fan across his face, the viscount fell off the platform and onto his face.

"You'll pay for this, Tavistoke!" shouted his new wife. She ground his hand with her heel as she spun around and stalked out of the ballroom.

Max and Tristram hopped down and helped their father rise. Nursing his hurt hand and pride, he hobbled after her, shouting, "Anne, my dear, wait! I didn't mean it! Wait for me!"

After two seconds of stunned silence, the entire ballroom erupted in uninhibited laughter.

Max turned to his brother and said, "It couldn't have turned out better, you know. Papa will be living under the cat's paw for the rest of his life. He will not have a chance to get into trouble."

"Well done, my boys," said the Marquess of Cravenwell, appearing from nowhere. "I couldn't have asked for a more amusing end to our little arrangement."

Tristram faced the old man and said stiffly, "I will have my solicitor bring you the balance of Papa's debt tomorrow, my lord."

The marquess waved his bony hand and shook his head. "No need. Lady Anne took care of all that this afternoon. You are released from any obligation to me."

Max held out his hand to the old man. After hesitating a second, the marquess shook it. "It has been a pleasure, gentlemen. Good-bye." With a bow to Philippa and Kate, who had appeared at their husbands' sides, the marquess turned and left the ball.

To everyone's surprise, both brothers gave a shout of laughter and threw their arms around their brides, kissing them thoroughly.

When they recalled their surroundings, Tristram said, "I'm glad we all realized the errors of our ways before it was too late. We very nearly had a tragedy on our hands instead of a comedy. What was it Shakespeare's Romeo said?"

"I do hope you are not expecting me to answer that, halfling," said Max.

Ignoring this, Tristram continued, "When all was lost, he said, 'I am Fortune's fool.' We very nearly were, too."

"Not you, little brother," said Max, cuffing Tristram on the arm. "You are the smart one in the family. Now, enough of this philosophizing. I much prefer waltzing with my beautiful wife. Kate, shall we waltz?"

"Forever and ever," she whispered, taking his arm and following him onto the dance floor once again.